lost without you

MIGNON MYKEL

ALSO BY MIGNON MYKEL

LOVE IN ALL PLACES *SERIES*
full series reading order

Interference **(Prescott Family)**
O'Gallagher Nights: The Complete Series
Troublemaker **(Prescott Family)**
Saving Grace
Breakaway **(Prescott Family)**
Altercation **(Prescott Family)**
27: Dropping the Gloves **(Enforcers of San Diego)**
32: Refuse to Lose **(Enforcers of San Diego)**
Holding **(Prescott Family)**
A Holiday for the Books **(Prescott Family)**
From the Beginning **(Prescott Family)**

Caught in the Act
Homewrecker
Lost Without You
For the First Time

Trust
(an Everyday Heroes world title)

Serendipity
(a Salvation Society world title)

lost without you

Copyright © 2020 by Mignon Mykel

All rights reserved.

No part of this publication may be reproduced, stored in or introduced into a media retrieval system or transmitted, in any form or by any means (electronic, mechanical, photocopying, recording or otherwise) without the prior written permission of the copyright owner and the publisher of this book, excepting of brief quotations for use in reviews.

This is a work of fiction. Names, characters, places, and incidents are the product of the author's imagination. Any resemblances to actual persons, living or dead, are entirely coincidental.

Cover Design and Formatting: oh so novel
Cover image photographer: Regina Wamba

Table of Contents

Prologue	9
Chapter One	16
Chapter Two	22
Chapter Three	31
Chapter Four	37
Chapter Five	46
Chapter Six	56
Chapter Seven	63
Chapter Eight	70
Chapter Nine	84
Chapter Ten	92
Chapter Eleven	98
Chapter Twelve	108
Chapter Thirteen	120
Chapter Fourteen	130
Chapter Fifteen	139
Chapter Sixteen	150
Chapter Seventeen	154
Chapter Eighteen	163
Chapter Nineteen	171
Chapter Twenty	177
Epilogue	180
What's Next?	187
From the Author	195
About Mignon Mykel	197

PROLOGUE

SAVANNAH

AGE 8

"Hi. I'm Ryan Madden."

I felt my face flare in a blush as the boy on the bike stopped, but I waved anyway, my hand up by my chest. "Hi, Ryan. I'm Savannah Slate."

My family and me just moved in to our new house yesterday, and I was drawing with chalk out front while my mom and dad unpacked more. We moved all the way across the country, in a trip that took three days and three different hotels.

My dad got a new job in California, and literally the day after school let out for the summer, we left Columbus, Ohio behind.

I didn't have any brothers or sisters, and back in Ohio I didn't really mind so much. I had lots of friends.

So, when we got to the new house yesterday and I saw the boy riding his bike up and down and around the cul de sac, I was maybe a little hopeful we could be friends.

"Hi, Savannah. I'm ten."

I stood up and wiped my chalk dusted hands on my jeans, leaving behind blue and pink powder. "I'm eight.

Almost nine. Well, in July."

Oh, I hoped I wasn't too young to be his friend. He was literally the only kid I saw yesterday and today. If he didn't want to be my friend because I was a baby, I'd be so bored this summer!

"Awesome. My birthday is next month too. I turn eleven. Do you have a bike?"

"I do!" It was one of the first things off the giant moving semi this morning. "Let me go ask my mom if I can ride."

"Cool."

And just like that, I had a friend. We rode bikes until the sun started to go down and the street lights came on.

AGE 12

I sighed heavily as the words in front of me seemed to scramble. I was recently diagnosed with dyslexia, but having a name to the issue didn't exactly help matters.

I was going to fail another test. I just knew it.

A sound at my window had me turning from my desk and moving around my bed, lifting the window of my second-story bedroom.

Down below, my best friend in the whole world—even more than Jenny Meiers—Ryan had his arm pulled back. When I opened the window though, he dropped his arm, and whatever was in his hand fell to the ground.

"Whatcha up to, Sav?"

Ryan was a freshman this year, and I wouldn't lie, I'd been afraid that he couldn't be friends with me anymore once he was a big bad high schooler.

And while we didn't hang out every day anymore, he still made time for me.

Leaning on my hands on the window sill, I sighed again.

"My stupid social studies homework. I failed my last test, and mom wasn't too happy with me." She didn't understand how I didn't do better now that we had a diagnosis and I got special treatment for tests.

If anything, taking tests away from the rest of my classmates made me more anxious.

Did they think I was getting special treatment?

Did they think I was a teacher's pet or something?

I forcefully cleared the anxious thoughts.

"Can you come out and hang with me?" Ryan put his hands in the pockets of his jeans, tipping his head to the side.

He needed a haircut.

The dark blond hair that fell over his forehead was nearly in his eyes, but he liked to swoosh his hair to the side. It was a thing that all the high school boys were doing.

Making a face, I shook my head. "I can't. I have my test tomorrow, and if I don't get an eight-two on it, mom says I'm grounded." An eighty-two would bring my class average up to passing.

Ryan's face pulled together in thought before he abruptly said, "All right. Catch you soon."

Frowning, I watched him leave the backyard, walking into his own, until he disappeared through the sliding door off the Madden family kitchen.

Suddenly sad, I pushed the window back down and returned to my desk, the threat of frustrated tears trying to take my attention away from the words in black and white. Even the now-normal sound of mom and dad's raised voices downstairs were adding to the growing anxiety.

They fought all the time, and many of their fights were about me and my inability to pass tests.

I wasn't sure how much longer I stared at the page in

front of me, but a knock at my bedroom door startled me out of my stupor.

"Yeah?"

The door pushed open and my dad was there. "How are you holding up, Savannah?"

My shoulders fell and I felt my entire body melt forward. "I'm frustrated. Nothing is making sense," I said, pointing to my textbook.

"How about you take a break? The Maddens invited you to dinner."

I sat up straight again, hope coursing through my body. "Can I?" It was a school night and typically, this wasn't allowed. I knew that this wasn't mom's idea.

"Absolutely. Just be home by eight. I talked to Ryan's parents so they know."

I jumped up from my desk chair and ran to my dad to give him a hug. "Thank you!"

His hug was strong, and he dropped his face to the top of my head to press a kiss in front of my messy pony tail. "Love you, kiddo."

The next three hours were just what I needed. Ryan and I played video games in the basement before dinner was ready. His mom made spaghetti and conversation flowed between school for me, the upcoming Freshman baseball season for him, and memories from the last few years.

After, Ryan and I went back downstairs to catch up on our favorite show, Two and a Half Men.

"Thank you for saving me," I finally said during a commercial. We sat on the opposite ends of the couch, and it took all of me to have the courage to turn my head to look at him.

I expected him to shrug it off like he normally would,

but instead when he looked at me, I felt like he *really* looked at me.

His gray eyes actually *saw* me.

And after what felt like ages, he answered, "You're my number one. You'll always be my number one. And if you need a break, I'll do what I can to give it to you."

That night, for the first time in weeks, I went to bed with a smile on my face.

AGAIN, AND AGAIN, AND AGAIN

The school year ended, and the next began.

Again, and again.

I failed more tests, but still managed to pass my classes.

My parents divorced, and my mom moved out, leaving me with my dad full-time. They never outwardly said it was because of me—my therapist even tried to convince me it couldn't be my fault—but I couldn't help but feel like I had a heavy hand in their failed marriage.

My one constant through it all though, was Ryan.

My best friend, through and through.

He saved me on more than one occasion, and any time I'd mentioned it, he repeated those words.

"You're my number one. Always will be."

When he was a senior in high school, to my sophomore, he even dumped a girlfriend who wasn't too happy with our friendship.

"You're my number one, Sav. Always will be."

Then, my own senior year, when my prom date no-showed me and I was left on my couch, all dressed up with nowhere to go, he drove the hour from college to sit on my couch with me.

Even danced with me in my living room.

"You're my number one."

Then there was *that* night.

My twenty-first birthday.

A drunken night in college town.

He took me to his favorite haunts.

We got wasted.

So wasted.

But I remembered every.

Single.

Moment.

Including the fear in the morning, naked in bed next to him, that our friendship would be ruined.

He was my best friend.

He was *my* number one.

And I didn't want that to change.

So I let my fear dictate my wants, and I pushed him away. "This can't go anywhere. It was a mistake. We were...drunk," I managed to croak out as I hurriedly pulled on my shirt and linen pants.

"Sav."

I shook my head. "No. No, Ryan. It cannot go anywhere. It was a mistake."

Maybe if I said it enough, that it was a mistake, I'd believe it.

Ryan slowly got out of his disheveled bed and grabbed his boxers, putting them on in an almost lazy way. I had to force myself to look away.

He walked me to the front door of his college apartment—just like all those years growing up, we were neighbors now, too—and hugged me. "I'm sorry, Savannah. You're my number one..."

I pushed him away with a sad smile, and avoided him the rest of the weekend.

Soon though, everything was back to normal.

Back to Ryan and Sav, best friends.

Ryan and Sav, neighbors once again, just in another new location.

There was a comfort in it. I knew where he was and I knew I could turn to him, even though I tried not to as much now. Not after sleeping with him. I didn't want to be...

Needy.

So, when one of his college baseball buddies signed him up for a reality dating show, I laughed.

And when he was casted for said dating show, I teased.

But when he told the single female vying for attention from the four remaining men on set that she was his number one?

Well then...

Then, I cried

CHAPTER ONE

SAVANNAH

The airport was deserted.

Yes, I'd thought twice about heading to my grandpa's cabin in Colorado Springs days after the United States started to freak out about coronavirus, but if we were headed in the same direction as China, and Italy, and Spain...

Then I wanted one last weekend away before being holed up in my apartment for who the hell knew how long.

I worked at a local Irish pub in San Diego, and we'd been needing to close early due to lack of staff and patrons. Closing time was brought up to eight because there just weren't enough people coming in. That alone told me the rumored quarantine was coming. Heck, even baseball spring training and the hockey season had been postponed yesterday!

I knew the lock down was only a matter of days away.

Some people were scared.

Some thought it was all a hoax.

Right now, I didn't know what I thought, but I did know that I needed just a little bit of time. A little bit of quiet.

A little bit of clean air.

I wanted a different level of alone than I got in my so-called "luxury" apartment complex.

The one where I could hear the footsteps over my head, and the wall-banging sex behind my bedroom wall.

The complex that was supposed to be a smoke-free place of living, but if I left my windows open for too long, my place smelled like I was the tobacco smoker.

Or, worse yet, the weed smoker.

Nothing against weed.

It just wasn't my favorite, and I preferred to not get a contact high.

After Monday's *The Rose* watch party with the Maddens and some of Ryan's closest baseball buddies—at what I now realized was likely my last group get-together for the foreseeable future—I decided I needed to get away.

Ryan's words to the up-and-coming actress had nothing to do with it.

None at all.

Maybe if I kept saying it, I'd believe it.

I mean...

Bella was perfect for him!

She was gorgeous, with long red hair.

Bright green eyes.

A sweet laugh.

And when she looked at Ryan, there was little doubt that he was her top choice.

The way she interacted with the other men was fine, but there was just something about how she laughed with, leaned into, *loved* my best friend.

He was going to move out of our apartment complex and start a life in Los Angeles. It was only a matter of time until he was no longer ten doors away. And if he moved to Los Angeles, he'd no longer work at O'Gallagher's, and even though we didn't work many of the same shifts, I still saw him in passing. If he moved, my only connection to him would be the phone, but I wasn't great with that. I left texts unanswered for days, and let's not even talk about how long it took me to listen to my voice mails.

I was going to lose my best friend.

To a beautiful redheaded Hollywood star.

"You're my number one," he said softly, his eyes not on Bella's face, but on his hand that rubbed the ends of her hair in an act that looked more intimate...

It was increasingly difficult to function as I thought about the direction of his life, so I pushed the replaying scenes from my head and got my rental car after lightly joking with the associate about how quiet the airport was. From there, I made the ninety minute drive away from the busy Denver area, into the just as busy Colorado Springs area. Fifteen minutes after hitting the city limits, and I was beating myself up for not upgrading my car selection.

The little forward-wheel drive economy car was having a hell of a time on the steep incline that lead to the remoteness of Grandpa's cabin. I'd been driving my all-wheel drive, six-cylinder sport utility for so long, that I forgot the difference in drivability. Thank goodness, the weather had been warmer this past week and there wasn't any lingering snow on the roads.

This time of year, you never did know what you were going to get out here in the mountains.

Being mid-March still meant snow storms were a possibility but, again, being mid-March also meant the weather could be nearly seventy the following day. One could joke that Colorado was bipolar in the spring, but if that was the case year after year, could you really expect anything different?

The paved road went further into the woods and shortly after mature trees and pines graced either side of the car, the pavement stopped abruptly. I slowed the car enough to drive over the bump between pavement and gravel, and drove the next mile in silence.

Gravel crunching under the tires.

The wind and nature coming through the two inch crack in my window.

I wasn't even at the cabin yet, and already I felt loads better.

This weekend was just what the doctor ordered.

Figuratively, I mean.

Turning left at the fork in the road, it was only two more minutes until I was at the one-room hunting cabin my Grandpa left to my dad years ago. My dad wasn't a hunter, but the land was still protected under our land agreement. I wondered if I'd see any deer this weekend, or just the typical rabbits who liked to hang out around the back.

I parked the car and grabbed my backpack from the passenger seat. The city girl in me locked the car doors still, even though I knew I wasn't going to see a single soul over the next seventy-two hours.

While it was only a one-room cabin, it was still fairly large.

For a cabin, anyway.

At four-hundred square feet, there was plenty of room for me and my lonesome.

That, and it had a generator, and I had a great data plan, so I could shamelessly Netflix and chill by myself. I planned on catching up on All American and The 100 this weekend, and maybe finish one of the docuseries that I'd been slowly getting through.

I walked up the old, rickety steps to the porch as I fished out my home keyring from the front of my backpack.

Between my car key and my mailbox key, was a silver key that would unlock my solidarity.

Like magic—or not, because it wasn't like anyone changed the locks since my dad gave me the key last summer—the key turned and the door swung open.

"Home sweet home," I murmured, stepping inside and closing the door behind me.

I dropped my backpack to the floor and took in the open space. There was firewood stacked by the fireplace on the wall to my right, and the bed was still dressed from the last stay. And, with the kitchen to my left, I realized that if there was any food still in the cabinets, it was probably way past expiration.

Longingly, I looked ahead toward the bathroom with— God, I hoped—running water. I really didn't want to go into the well, but I knew how to if it came down to it. I'd do anything to wash my face right now, but I knew I had other things to do first.

I was going to have to go back down and into town for food, but also to wash linens.

The last thing I wanted to do was spend two hours at a laundromat, but I also wasn't about to sleep in a dusty bed.

Plan in place, I knelt in front of my backpack to pull out my wallet before placing my bag on a wooden rocking chair by the fireplace.

Then, I quickly stripped the bed and rolled it up into

one giant ball, managing to juggle it in my right arm as I grabbed my wallet and two sets of keys in my left hand.

Back on the porch, I used the closed door to hold the linens up as I re-locked the entrance, before making my way back to my rental.

Down to town I go.

CHAPTER TWO

RYAN

If there was one person I was thankful for, right here, right now, right this second...

It was Jackson Slate.

For six weeks, I'd been holed up at his father's hunting cabin in Colorado Springs, as I waited for *The Rose* to finish airing.

Because I made it to the final two, I was under contract to not be seen out in public. It had been, God, ten, twelve years? Since I'd been at this cabin with my best friend and her family, but it was the first place I thought of when I found out I had to be in seclusion until I was due back to film the finale episode.

Spoiler alert, I won the damn thing.

Another spoiler?

I told Bella no.

How the hell could I go through with a relationship with her—hell, a *marriage*—when I constantly saw someone else when I looked at her?

It wasn't Bella's red hair I watched my hands sift through.

It wasn't Bella's green eyes I focused on.

I mean, yeah, sure, in the physical, yes, it was Bella.

But it wasn't Bella I was seeing.

It was a spunky brunette with brown eyes, who'd had my heart since I was fucking ten years old. Talk about a piss-poor moment to realize the love you had for your best friend wasn't going anywhere, no matter how hard you tried.

On a television show that had the highest ratings of any reality show.

A show that I'd hoped would shake the feelings that Savannah Slate inspired.

So, not only did I have to go basically underground while the show finished airing, because it wouldn't do the show any favors for one of their top contenders to be seen around town, but also because I was the first guy in the show's history to say "no" when all was said and done.

I'd told the producers my intentions before they set me up on the Hawaiian shore, and they tried to convince me to say yes.

To try.

To put on another media circus for a couple of months.

But all I could think, all I could remember, all I could *see*, was the morning after Savannah's twenty-first birthday, and the look of absolute pain on her face as she told me we were a mistake.

Basically, that I was a lapse in judgement.

That she'd been too drunk to know better.

As if I didn't know her better than that.

But I let her have her thoughts.

I let her push me away.

I gave her her space and eventually, took back her friendship.

We never truly got back to what we were, but it wasn't

for my lack of trying. If I had to guess, it was the whirlwind of thoughts that had a habit of taking over Savannah's mind.

Knowing that that one night—one of the best nights of my life—was the reason our friendship faltered...

I knew I had to do something. I knew that the longer I stayed around Savannah—at work, at the apartment complex, at holiday dinners—the more I wanted to take that night back.

No, not take it back.

Redo the morning after.

But I couldn't go back and change how everything went down. Instead, I was left with the feeling that I loved a woman who would never allow me to love her in the way she most deserved.

So, when my buddy and roommate Mitch signed me up for *The Rose* as a joke, and I actually was casted, I took it as a sign.

A sign that it was time to move on.

I couldn't keep hanging around Savannah, hoping she'd see that we could be more than friends—and be *good* at being more than friends.

Couldn't keep hoping for another night like July, twenty-sixteen.

Couldn't keep hoping for *more*.

Dating and casual hook ups weren't working for me, and I'd tried. Instead, removing myself from San Diego seemed like the best option.

Clearly, it hadn't been.

Shaking my head, I tiredly watched the road turn from asphalt to gravel, and the rumble below the tires nearly lulled me into peace.

Nearly.

Thoughts of Savannah never let me have full, true peace.

The trip down the gravel road seemed shorter and shorter each time I took it, and once I was at the old hunter's cabin, I shut off the engine and grabbed my bag of food from the seat, as well as the five-pound bag of ice from the passenger floorboard.

I tried to make the trip into town only once a week, but for a guy who lived a fairly high-in-produce life, I was getting sick of the carbs. Lettuce wouldn't keep in the ice chest, so outside of pasta and soup, I was pretty limited to what I could eat. This week, I had apples and bananas. Maybe next week, I'd grab oranges.

Or, maybe I'd get apples and bananas again.

...*I'd probably get apples and bananas again*, I thought with a sigh.

I walked up the three wooden steps to the front door, and turned the knob.

It was locked.

Frowning, I rearranged my bags to get my keys out. I thought I'd left the door unlocked when I left, but at this point, who the hell knew?

My days all ran together, and I was waiting impatiently for the call that gave me flight instructions for the reunion finale show. It was originally scheduled for the upcoming week, but the producers were being slow on when to bring me back to Los Angeles. My last communication with them was that, at the latest, I'd fly into LAX on Monday morning.

There were a lot of fears in the world right now, with the emerging coronavirus, and there was even talk about doing the show remotely.

As long as I could be back at my house in San Diego before anything serious went down in the country, I'd be happy.

Inside the cabin, I immediately went to the kitchen area with my bags and started to unpack the groceries. Once everything was where I wanted it, I brought the bag of ice to the large cooler I'd been using, and, after pulling out the egg carton, added the ice on top of the remaining contents.

Block cheese, eggs, water.

The eggs and lid back in place, I stood and turned around—and stared at the bed.

What in the...?

Where the hell did the linens go?

Frowning, my long gait carried me to the other side of the cabin as my eyes scanned the four hundred square feet surrounding me for any type of clue.

It was then that my eyes landed on the old, familiar backpack, and not only did my feet falter, but my heart did too.

I knew that backpack.

It had come along on a number of trips over the last ten years.

A trusty, old school JanSport with sewn on patches from different state parks we'd hiked.

Which only meant one thing.

Savannah was here.

She was here.

In Colorado Springs.

The sound of tires on gravel had me looking out the window and sure enough, a car came through the clearing. It obviously slowed upon seeing my rental.

Not wanting to delay the inevitable—and not wanting to scare the hell out of her—I went to greet my best friend out on the porch.

Her gaze met mine through the windshield and fuck if it didn't hurt that she didn't smile at seeing me.

Once upon a time, we were thick as thieves. She may have been two years younger than me, but from the day I saw her drawing nonsense with chalk on her driveway, she'd been my single constant.

Sure, there was my family, my friends, school...then college, and baseball.

God, baseball took up so much of my life.

Even now, coaching high school baseball, the sport was still a major part of who I was.

But never was anything greater than Savannah, whether she was pushing me away—three years ago or five months ago when I last saw her—or whatever it was she was doing by being here with me this weekend.

Not wanting things to be awkward, I moved down the steps toward her car, just as she opened the door.

"Hey, stranger," I said lightly.

I watched a myriad of emotions cross her beautiful face, before she finally settled on a smile.

With her arms thrown out wide, she stepped close and I took the hug she was offering.

"What are you doing here?" she asked in the same jovial tone she used when she told me goodbye months ago, and I tried to ignore the kick in the gut I felt at the knowledge she hadn't known I was here.

It was simply a coincidence.

I refrained from dropping my nose to her coconut-scented hair and instead, forced myself to step away from her embrace. "Hiding out for a few weeks. What are you doing here?"

"I wanted to get away. Needed some quiet. Life..." She shook her head and smiled again—not that it was a true smile. It didn't make the dimple just under her left eye pop. "It's just been crazy, and I wanted to get away before I couldn't anymore."

"What do you mean, 'couldn't anymore'?"

She laughed and turned to open the back of the car. "Are you living fully off the grid, Ryan? Where have you been? There's talk about stay-at-home orders in California." My brows lifted. I knew that it was happening in other countries, but no, I hadn't heard that my home state was considering the order. However, I also knew Savannah well enough to know she was clearly deflecting right now. "Speaking of off the grid," she continued, "where were you when I got here?"

I watched as she reached in and pulled out the missing, but now clean and folded, bed linens. I reached for them to help, as I answered her. "I went to town for groceries and coffee. There's a place that couldn't care less that I'm there."

This time, the smile she gave me was real. "Aw, is the celebrity life getting hard for you? You need to hide out? How far ahead is your life from the show airing, anyway?"

"I've been here for six weeks, but the finale is due to film on Monday, so I was going to head back to California then. And no, celebrity life isn't hard, but I'm not supposed to be answering questions. So yes, I need to hide."

Savannah bent further in the car and my eyes travelled

down her long-sleeved cotton shirt on her back, to her ass in skin-tight denim. I shifted on my feet before taking a step back.

I couldn't tell you the first time that I noticed-noticed Savannah, but man, since then I was hit with every damn emotion whenever she was near.

When she emerged from the car, she had her own bag of groceries. "So, is Bella here with you?" One brown brow was raised as she looked at me, and I couldn't read much of her expression.

Did she want Bella here?

"I mean, I'm not like...ruining some sex fest or something, right?" She added a small laugh but moved past me quickly. I followed her up the stairs and reached for the door before she could, pushing it open for her.

"Nope, just me." I didn't elaborate.

If she really wanted to know more, she'd ask.

Savannah wasn't afraid to ask the hard questions.

At least, she never used to be.

"Well, that's good, I guess. I have no issues sharing a bed with you, but I'm not really all about sharing a bed with you love birds."

Savannah busied herself with the contents of her bag, but I saw the flush on her face, and how the red dropped down her neck and through the neck of her shirt.

She was affected.

Good.

Suddenly, what once looked like another boring weekend was looking up.

I was going to get back in Savannah's good graces—no, she never once outwardly told me we were on the outs, but our friendship had been strained since her twenty-first birthday.

Strained because she pushed me away.

Strained because I was fighting—and losing—the battle of being in love with my best friend.

Coincidence or not that we were both here for a weekend, I was going to do everything I could to mend what was broken.

And hopefully, before the end of it, make her realize she loved me too.

Yeah, the weekend didn't look so bleak anymore.

CHAPTER THREE

SAVANNAH

Good God, did I really just say that?

That I didn't mind being in a bed with him, but, oh, heaven forbid, there were three of us in it? And what the hell was up with me and thinking—*talking*—about him and sex?

Because, like Pavlov's dog, every time I put *sex* and *Ryan* in the same thought, my heart squeezed, my lungs couldn't appropriately fill with air, and a feeling of dread washed over me.

Which was a funny feeling, when paired next to the one of excitement at seeing him for the first time in nearly five months.

Since the going away party at the apartment he shared with Mitch Tennyson.

The night before I was supposed to drive him the airport.

The night I told Mitch that I had an unexpected obligation come up, and couldn't do it anymore. Could he drive Ryan instead?

I effectively avoided Ryan the rest of that night, outside of a hug goodbye with words of good luck.

God, I couldn't believe he was here.

Why didn't my dad tell me!

Because, surely, my dad was the one who offered the cabin to Ryan.

You didn't tell Dad you were coming, my subconscious was quick to remind, and I scolded that devil on my shoulder.

I pulled out a bunch of bananas that were more on the side of green, and the bag of Halo oranges, and put both on the counter next to the yellow bananas and apples that Ryan must have bought earlier.

We had to have just missed each other this morning.

I couldn't believe my timing...

Here I was, running away from home and the memories of him on television, making out with Bella and giving her words that he always told me, and low and behold, here he was.

Right here.

Where I was trying to hide.

Guess there was no hiding from Ryan.

Never really had been.

He'd always known when I needed him.

Knew when I needed a friend.

Knew when I needed a distraction.

And knew when I needed space.

But one thing he didn't seem to know, was that I needed him.

Just...

Needed *him*.

I'd needed him three and a half years ago to tell me that I was being stupid. To pull me back into his arms and talk sense into me.

But he didn't.

He let me walk away.

He let me hide.

And eventually, he let me pretend that night never happened.

I was nearly convinced that that night truly meant more to me than it did to him.

You told him to forget it.

Fucking devil.

Shut the hell up.

"You okay over there?" Ryan asked from the bed, as he tucked the flat sheet into the bottom of the bed. "You're making some noises over there. Kind of sound like a dying cat."

"Ha ha." I rolled my eyes. God, I hoped I wasn't talking out loud. Sometimes when the thoughts were rolling... "Just have a lot on my mind. I didn't realize my thoughts were so loud."

"They're not, but you're grunting and taking your anger out on the fruit." I knew he was joking, but I eyed the fruit all the same. Meanwhile, he pulled the sheet up to the already dressed pillows. "I'm getting the feeling that my being here is interfering with whatever you came here for, so I'm sorry. Truly. I'd offer to go but...I don't really have anywhere else to go right now." His muscles bunched and stretched as he grabbed the quilt my grandmother sewed many, many years ago, and tossed it flat on the bed, before straightening it.

"No," I shook my head. "No, it's fine. You're fine. It'll just be like old times. And you can tell me all about your Hollywood stint." I didn't really want to hear about how wonderful Bella was, but hey, that's what best friends did, right?

Support one another?

"Surely you don't want the show spoiled..."

Was he teasing me? I couldn't see his face, but I could hear a smile on his voice.

"The suspense is killing me, yeah," I tried teasing back. "I'd like to know if I need to expect Bella at Christmas dinner this year. I'll need to up my hair salon routine if so." It was a running joke that I should visit a salon more often, but my hair was long and I had scissors...

I could cut a straight line.

And when the desire for bangs arose, I was pretty damn good at them.

Besides, my hair was up in a pony tail or braids or bun all the time. I didn't really care if I had a stylish haircut.

But if I had to break bread with a beautiful actress...

My dad and I did Christmas with the Madden family every year, and so far, I'd been lucky—no girlfriends, famous or otherwise.

I wasn't naïve in thinking he'd never had a girlfriend, or that he didn't have a fuck buddy here or there. The man was gorgeous.

Tall, at somewhere over six-feet. Easily a foot taller than my five-three frame.

Built, but not gross muscle-building built.

Personable. He was friends with damn near everyone, which really only made the package a-thousand times better.

And, as much as I tried not to remember, he was...

Considerate...

In bed.

I mean, what woman wouldn't want to hold on to him?

Sure, he could tease relentlessly, and yeah, he sometimes chewed his gum with his mouth open—a hazard from his baseball years—but really, who didn't have faults?

So while yes, I knew he had women, he'd always been kind enough to not flaunt them in front of me. Times changed though, and with the rumors swirling from *The Rose* and the looks I saw with my own two eyes...

Would this year be the year of the fiancée?

My heart cracked at the thought.

Ryan stood, and even with the bed and a few feet of floor between us, I could see the calculations in his eyes.

What was he thinking?

What was he picturing?

How he was going to formally introduce me to the love of his life?

Or maybe, he wouldn't. Women didn't take too kindly to female best friends.

Oh, God.

I was going to lose my best friend.

My heart started to race as fast as my thoughts, but not until after it felt like a vise tightened around the muscle.

It had been many years since I'd experienced a full-fledged anxiety attack and now was so not the time for this one.

"Savannah."

This was my last time to spend any sort of time with my best friend.

I'd wasted so many years, being stupid and holding him at arm's length.

So, so many years.

Now, not only was my heart racing, but my breathing had accelerated too.

"Sav." His hands were on my shoulders and my eyes

snapped up to his. When did he get right here?

"You're all right, Sav. Just breathe. Slowly."

And just like so many years ago, he brought me into his arms and ran a hand up and down my back slowly in a cadence I could mimic with my breaths. "Breathe, Savvy. You're good."

That crack in my heart was growing, but I was good at hardening myself.

I recovered from a major broken heart at twenty-one. I could push past this chipping away now, at twenty-four.

We stood like that for what had to be five minutes, before he stopped talking calming words to me, and instead went back to the previous conversation—something he never shied from.

"One, you're beautiful, Savannah. Bella doesn't hold a candle next to you."

I scoffed and tried to push back from him, but he held tight.

"And two...I'm not with Bella."

CHAPTER FOUR

RYAN

The first time Savannah had a panic attack, we were walking home from the middle school.

She'd worked herself up into a full frenzy before school even ended, all over a bad test score, and the normally fifteen minute walk home took nearly thirty minutes. I didn't know what the right thing to do was, but I attempted breathing with her.

She would calm down, we'd walk a little further, and she'd be in a full-blown panic attack all over again.

It would be another year before I learned that her mom was borderline mentally abusive and even when I figured it out, it was just that—*I* figured it out.

Savannah didn't tell me outright, but I pieced the puzzle together.

When her parents divorced, I knew that Savannah blamed herself.

That time, I knew because she *did* tell me.

If only she were smarter.

If only she didn't get so nervous that the words got mixed up.

If only...

I grew up with incredibly supportive parents, so I had

no idea how her mom could be the way she was. Even now, years later, I knew Savannah spoke with her mom rarely, and saw her even less.

What I gathered though, was her mom didn't handle her anxiety attacks well, which was a sick sort of puzzle in itself.

Savannah had anxiety attacks because of fears she wasn't good enough. Fears of disappointing her mom. But regardless, her mom was seemingly disappointed in her, which only brought on bigger anxiety attacks.

Something I was sure her mom had no clue of—but she would have if she'd taken the time to actually *look* at her daughter—was that there were different levels to the attacks.

First, there was the quiet.

Savannah could be smiling and joking one minute, and then just...

Go quiet.

Out of nowhere.

And typically, people didn't notice because the conversation changed, or the commercial switched to the show, or someone else came and took the person's attention away from her.

Then, there was the fidgeting. She'd hold her hands in front of her, pinching the skin between her index finger and thumb, or fold her fingers together and squeeze.

After that, her breathing would pick up. Every now and then, you could hear her trying to calm herself by taking a single deep breath, but if that didn't work, the tears were next.

I hated when it got to the tears.

So, to try to stay away from the tears, I always went with comedy—and even if she really hadn't been throwing the bananas around this time, the comment made her stop and look.

It made her stop and think.

Stop and *breathe*.

But while I got her to that point, where she was breathing, I also knew it was never that easy. Never that quick to stop.

Whatever train her thoughts were on always found another turn, and she worked herself up all over again.

So if comedy didn't stop the runaway train, I held her, and having her here in my arms was never a hardship. I'd do anything to get her out of the current spiral her mind was on.

It killed me a little inside though when she tried to pull away.

"I'm not with Bella," I repeated, thinking she maybe hadn't heard me but still trying to keep her close.

Part of me wanted to see her facial expression.

See how she was reacting to that news.

But the other part of me was scared she wouldn't react in the way I wanted her to.

I was still that week-shy of twenty-three years old kid, who watched his best friend take the walk of shame after a night that could never be shameful.

God, I'd been so stupid.

Stupid to let her walk away.

Stupid to let her stay away.

Stupid to think that time could ease the ache.

Or, my ultimate stupidity, to think that a reality dating show could magically cure me.

Savannah tried pushing away again and this time I loosened my arms enough for her to look up at me. She stared hard, her brown eyes searching mine, before she stammered, "B-but *why*? She loved you!"

And I love you, I thought, but knew better than to voice. Now was not the time to confess my feelings.

Hell, I wasn't sure there ever was going to be a time, but as long as she stayed here this weekend, I could test the waters. Get back in her good graces.

"It wouldn't have worked," I answered instead. "Her schedule, her lifestyle... It wasn't what I wanted."

Slowly, she shook her head, the look of confusion still all over her face. "I just...don't get you, sometimes."

Clearly.

"You better?" I forced myself to drop my arms from her, and she nodded.

"I am. Thank you. I don't know where my head went." She looked away as she said it, as if she could lie to me.

As if I hadn't walked her through numerous attacks in the past.

If she wanted to pretend, I'd let her.

For now.

"What's your plan?" I changed the subject. "Did you have anything riveting on the calendar for the weekend?" Stepping away from her felt like the stretching of an elastic.

Close to snapping.

But not actually breaking.

I moved to the cooler and knelt, pulling out a water bottle. I held it up and lifted a brow in a silent asking. She nodded and stepped closer, reaching for the bottle, and after, I grabbed a second for myself.

"Honestly, I was looking forward to just hanging out in bed, catching up on Netflix. But that was before... You know. Before I knew you were here. I can't believe my dad didn't mention it *once* in the...how many weeks did you say you were here? Six?"

I cracked the top of the water bottle and nodded. "Yeah. Just about."

"That's a long time to be by yourself. You're such a social guy."

She wasn't lying. In high school, I was the athlete and with that, came a fairly large social circle. Then, collegiate baseball brought a whole new social circle.

My parents had always expected me to go into some sort of career that my personality would work with. Bartending at O'Gallagher's wasn't exactly what they were thinking, but it paid well enough. It also gave me that social piece I craved, while giving me the occasional shift with the best friend who avoided me but pretended it was just a scheduling conflict.

So I bartended for the money, and coached for the joy, and never felt like I was truly working. Unlike Savannah's mom, my parents were supportive with any direction I took.

I could remember the last panic attack Savannah had in my presence, and it had to do with a "wasted degree" and "unnecessary student loans."

Her mother's words, I'd never doubted.

While her mother was a Class A bitch, her dad was always the reason why I knew Savannah was safe in her house. If Jackson loved one thing in life, it was his daughter.

Which was why, after Conor O'Gallagher offered me a job at the bar he owned—his son Aiden was one of my

Freshman baseball players and I met with all of my prospective players during their eighth grade year—I brought the idea of her working at the bar to Jackson.

Savannah may joke that I was the social one, but she was too. People loved her.

She was easy to talk to, and had a smile that lit up a room.

And she was really great at multitasking, something that made her a rockstar behind the pine bar top.

Knowing that my mind had gone off on a tangent, I finally answered Savannah's comment. "Eh, it gave me some time to think." Not a lie.

In six weeks, I replayed not only the last weeks over in my head, but I thought about every single misstep I took where Savannah was concerned. There had to be a reason why she was on the forefront of my mind when I was seconds away from telling another woman that I could see myself falling in love with her.

Actually, I knew the reason now.

Hell, I knew the reason then.

But not knowing where Savannah stood put hell on a guy's ego.

Savannah went to her backpack and placed it on the ground before sitting in the old rocker. Taking her lead, I moved closer and sat at the end of the bed so that our toes nearly touched—and every time she rocked gently, our knees *did* touch.

"That's why I came here," she admitted. "To think."

I recalled what she'd said earlier, and tried to get her to elaborate. "What's crazy at home? You said life was crazy."

She laughed and shook her head, but it looked forced.

"Dude. You really need to watch the news."

I wasn't going to let her skirt whatever she was hiding with that again. "No, no. Not the world. You. You can think about a global pandemic at home. Why did you need to fly to the mountains?"

Her smile was tight as she shook her head, lifting the water bottle to her lips, ineffectively trying to stop the conversation by taking a drink of water.

When she was through, she wiped the back of her hand over her mouth. "Why didn't you win the show? All the tabloids say you were the shoo-in. Hell, TMZ even broke that they heard you *did* win."

"Savannah." It was getting more and more clear that she was hiding something.

"And I saw how she looked at you." She nodded a few times and pointed the top of her water bottle in my direction. "Bella knew at *least* three weeks ago that you were her choice. Well...three episodes ago. However long ago that was."

"You want to talk about Bella?"

She held her hands out to her sides. "Clearly. I want to know what happened!"

I stared at her, trying to read her expression.

Exasperated.

Maybe a little annoyed.

Confused.

It was the confusion that had me contemplating the answer.

Could I tell her the truth?

Jack Nicholson's voice echoed loudly in my head: *You can't handle the truth!*

Right. I honestly didn't think she was ready for the truth.

"What was your obligation the morning of my flight?" I countered, which she was not expecting by the expression on her face. If my hunch was correct, she hadn't wanted to see me off because she cared.

And I was holding on tightly to that thought.

"Wh-what?"

Yeah, that stumble confirmed it but I knew better than to smile in victory. Instead, I repeated the question. "What was your obligation the day you were supposed to bring me to the airport?"

Her mouth worked but she couldn't get any words out.

"What was your hesitation in applying at the bar?" Yet another time she had to think twice before acting, when twenty-year-old Savannah would have jumped at the opportunity.

I knew damn well the reason why she dragged her feet in applying to be a bartender was me. Just like I knew that she'd asked to have as many opposite shifts as me as she could—which I knew because the O'Gallagher siblings wanted to be sure that there wasn't going to be any drama on their floor, and brought the request back to me.

"I didn't hesitate." Her brows were down and she crossed her arms, as well as one leg of the other.

Closing herself off.

Bringing herself in.

"You did. It took you over a week to drop off your application, and then when you were offered the job, you had to think about it for another week."

"I had...obligations." Then, when she must have

realized she used the same word I'd used earlier, she shook her head and looked away.

"You worked at Trader Joes."

"And I loved my co-workers. I loved my job." Her defenses were starting to rise, and I had to decide how much further I wanted to push.

Pushing too hard wouldn't do me any good, but backing off too quickly could be just as detrimental.

Especially when I was slowly getting the bigger picture.

She may have said it was a mistake. She may have pushed me away.

But that night affected her.

And I was starting to think that it hit her as hard as it hit me.

CHAPTER FIVE

SAVANNAH

Once Ryan was finished with his "twenty questions, Ryan edition," I excused myself to the bathroom.

After locking the door—a habit I did even in my own apartment when no one else was around—I flipped on the water and braced my arms on the sink, avoiding my reflection.

What did *any* of that have to do with Bella? The show?

What was he trying to do?

I looked up then to stare into my own brown eyes, trying to see whatever it was he saw as he pushed, but all I saw was bleakness staring back at me. It was that bleakness that told me if I stared too hard, too long, then I'd be well on my way to a new train of negative thoughts.

Not wanting to go there, I splashed water on my face, before reaching for the travel-sized bar soap that sat in a dish. I always felt better after cleaning my face, and this time was no different.

When I was through, when I had the hand towel pressed to my face, I inhaled deeply and held my breath.

Centering myself.

Satisfied, I put the towel back, looked at my reflection again, and nodded once.

I had this.

Exiting the bathroom, I was surprised to find the cabin empty.

Frowning, I moved toward the door. "Ryan?"

I opened the door, but he wasn't immediately there. "Ryan?" I tried again, my voice louder. Both rental cars sat idle and empty, so I knew he hadn't left.

To my right came a rustling in the leaves, but when I looked, there was nothing.

Was it a rabbit?

Or a deer?

Neither of which posed any sort of threat.

"Ryan!"

Shoot, where did he go? It wasn't like I was in the bathroom that long.

Crossing my arms, I looked around once more before frowning, taking myself back inside. He probably went for a walk, but who knew what direction he'd gone in. I wasn't about to go traipsing around the woods to try and find him.

I'd just sit and wait.

I dragged the rocking chair to the door and, using the chair to prop it open, sat down in the middle of the doorway. I was only sitting for thirty seconds before I was up on my feet again, back in the cabin, and grabbing my phone from the counter.

If I was going to sit and wait, I was going to try to pass a few levels of Candy Crush.

I'd recently had to restart my account, so I was only on level eight-hundred fifteen. Thankfully, I was good at seeing patterns before they appeared, and fairly quickly, I was up thirty levels and only down one life.

But any time I was on a winning streak and then lost, I immediately found myself bored with the game, and another loss of life just didn't sound interesting.

I shifted on the wooden rocker, bringing my foot up so my heel was on the edge of the chair, and rested my forearm on my knee. Now to waste time, I thumbed through Instagram, but after mindlessly double-tapping pretty pictures, I was bored there too.

Next stop in boredom busters?

Facebook.

Now that...

That could be a time suck.

The majority of posts were about toilet paper.

Or, lack thereof.

I looked away from the screen, and stared off to the right as I thought about my bathroom and under sink storage. If I remembered correctly, there were at least three rolls there.

My head swayed side to side as I contemplated...

You know those memes about being unable to keep your negative thoughts from your face?

Yeah. That was me.

If I saw an ugly shirt at Kohls, there was no hiding my feelings from my face.

So now, while contemplating my toilet paper situation, I knew that my thoughts were written all over my expression. Thank goodness, no one was around.

Either way, three rolls should last me five weeks minimum. I'd be good.

Bringing my attention back to Facebook, I scrolled more.

I was scrolling fast now, not even truly paying attention to what was being posted, but something caught my eye and I stopped, slowly scrolling back up to try and figure out what it was.

It was only three or so posts before I found what had caught my attention—a media day photo of Ryan.

From the photoshoot before the show began.

The producers were playing the bartender angle, and had him leaning against a bar top with a white bar towel over one shoulder. He had a five-o'clock shadow and his hair was messy but styled that way.

It was very "Ryan."

Laid back.

Good time.

Ryan.

I clicked the link that was attached to the image, curious.

The thing about *The Rose* and Ryan was, I didn't even need click-bait headlines to want to know what people had to say.

Ryan *was* the click-bait.

Unfortunately, this article had nothing of interest in it. In fact, the first paragraphs weren't even about Ryan at all!

Just as I was about to go back to Facebook though, a video appeared at the bottom of the article.

My thumb floated above the play button. The freeze screen was *that* scene.

The one that broke my heart.

I stared at the screen, not allowing my thumb to drop on the 'play' icon.

I knew what watching the scene again would do to me

and frankly...I didn't want to go there right now.

With a huge push of determination, I closed out of the app all together and looked out at the woods. The afternoon sun was starting to sink and once again, I worried about where my friend was.

"Duh," I said aloud. "You have your phone. Call him."

But shortly after hitting his contact, I heard his phone—from inside the cabin.

"Stupid boy." The scolding words were soft and obviously did no good, as said stupid boy wasn't around to hear them.

I checked the time, starting to get worried. Where did he go?

Maybe something happened to him.

Maybe he slipped and fell down a cliff.

Maybe he—

No. I shook my head, warding off thoughts.

For all my desires to be away from home and have quiet, it wasn't doing me much good. Not when the anxiety had managed to creep back into my life.

I'd been doing so damn good with the anxious thoughts and patterns, and here I was, starting to spiral all over again.

Well, I couldn't just sit here any longer.

Standing abruptly, I pushed the rocker back through the threshold and shut the door, ready to take off into the woods.

There was a small path that started off the trek, and I knew that eventually it would die off. I'd worry about the "what next" when I got to it.

Leaves and twigs crunched under my shoes as I made my way down the path. Above, the spring birds were singing, and the wind whistled through the trees. Although there was the occasional patch of snow that shade trees blocked from the sun, the recent fifties had brought a springtime feel to the woods.

A small breeze guided me further down the path and, for the first time since driving up and seeing Ryan, a sense of peace washed through me.

Suddenly, I knew exactly where Ryan had gone.

Once upon a time, we had a thinking spot out here.

Ryan had only been to the cabin with my dad and me a handful of times, but during one of our last trips—right after my high school graduation—we found a small creek in a clearing that hadn't been much larger than twelve feet across.

Sure that that was where I'd find my friend, I turned left at the end of the path.

Now, the walk wasn't as clear, and there were more roots and downed trees to step over, but if I listened closely, I could hear the gentle trickle of water.

A few more feet and a right turn later, and I could see him through the trees, sitting on a boulder.

Not bothering to be quiet—or loud, for that matter—I stepped through the tree line. "I was worried about you."

He looked over his shoulder, clearly not surprised to see me. Honestly, he looked like he'd been expecting me...and I had no idea why I thought that.

Or why my heart sped up at the prospect.

"Do you remember when we first found this spot?" He turned back toward the creek, and I moved closer, taking a seat on the boulder next to him after he moved over enough to give me room.

"Interestingly enough, I was just remembering. I'd actually forgotten about this spot."

"It's my favorite spot up here."

We sat in silence for a moment before he continued. "It was right before your nineteenth birthday."

"It was after my high school graduation," I opposed, because we didn't come for my birthday, but because I'd graduated with a B average.

I didn't look at him, but knew that if I did, I'd find the left side of his mouth kicked up in a crooked grin.

"Regardless, it was June."

"Well, we weren't here for my birthday. We were here for my graduation."

I felt him turn his head toward me and this time, I did look at him. His grin was wide as he shook his head. "Always gotta argue. Fine. We were here for your graduation."

"And maybe also because you guys won the NCAA championship. In Omaha, Nebraska." I only added the location because I liked to say it.

Oh-ma-hawww.

I smiled and looked back to the water.

"That was a good summer."

I nodded in agreement. It had been a good summer. I'd been excited to get into my program at the same college Ryan went to. I had so many plans for those next four years...

I tipped my head to the side as I thought about those plans again, and how it had been a struggle, but I met them. I got my fancy English degree, the one that proved that I was smart and that I could read and the words didn't necessarily jumble when I was focused and not stressed.

The trouble with fancy English degrees though is that

they don't always open up a world of possibilities. Not like, say, an accounting degree.

Or something more practical, like a Bachelors in Nursing.

Speaking of nursing...

"Are you even going to have a place to go back to, when you decide to go back to San Diego?" I looked at him after I posed the question, and he turned his head, frowning.

"Why wouldn't I? Mitch didn't say anything about subleasing or whatever. I told him I'd be back. Our lease is up next month anyway, so we talked about if the need arose, I'd just not resign the new lease."

After undergrad and baseball, Mitch went on to start medical school and was now a resident at the local teaching hospital. His current unit rotation—from what I gathered on the Facebook, because I really didn't talk to him much without Ryan around—was in an intensive care unit.

If things ended up going in the direction that was predicted...

"I was just thinking about Mitch, and the virus, and all the isolation stuff. That's all."

"Eh. Worst case scenario, I'll just bunker down with you."

He *clearly* didn't think there'd be an issue with that.

But there *clearly* was an issue with that.

"I'm cool with sharing a bed with you this weekend, but I don't have room for you in my apartment."

"I'll take the couch."

"You know damn well it's a cheap Ikea model."

He grimaced. "Yeah. That was a bitch to put together."

There was nothing quite as fun—sarcasm—as finding way

too many extra pieces after putting a piece of furniture together, and going back to be sure everything was put together correctly.

"Maybe Bella..." I still couldn't believe he lost the show! Surely, there was some dramatic twist that would make ratings soar, and then at the reunion show, Ryan would realize his errors.

"We are not talking about Bella," he interrupted. "At least, not until you answer my other questions."

"Ugh."

"Yeah. Ugh is right," he teased, and I had a really hard time ever holding a mad when he teased.

Sighing, I stood and said, "Well. I was just worried about you and needed to know where you were. I'm going to head back up."

"I'll go with you. I'm good now."

Quietly, we made our way back through the woods and up to the cabin, me leading the way. Ryan's steps were fairly in tune with mine and once again, I found peace in these woods.

The silence continued until we were both up the stairs and I was pushing through the door.

"You want to go into town for dinner?" Ryan asked.

"I really hadn't been planning on spending much money outside of the essentials," I said honestly. "I grabbed some Ready Pasta at the grocery store and was just going to cook that up and make buttered noodles for dinner tonight and tomorrow."

"Who eats buttered noodles?" Ryan shut the door and followed me into the kitchen area.

"Um, a lot of people." I frowned at him. "Who *doesn't* eat

buttered noodles? Add a dash of Italian seasonings and, viola. Excellence in a dish."

"More like bland in a dish. Let me take you to dinner. I am in dire need of real food. I haven't eaten out at all this week, and you being here calls for celebration."

"Now you're just making things up."

"Hey," he held his hands out, "I'll call it whatever to get a full-course meal."

"Fine. But I'm eating buttered noodles tomorrow. For lunch *and* dinner."

He made a gagging face, but agreed.

CHAPTER SIX

RYAN

The rest of the day was basically normal.

We ate.

We joked.

We reminisced.

Everything was like pre-sex Savannah and Ryan.

We were "just" Savannah and Ryan. Ryan and Savannah. Best friends who knew everything about one another.

Conversation was easy. There weren't any of those pretenses that seemed to fill the air in the recent years.

Maybe Savannah had been right—she just needed the clean and clear that Colorado brought her because the Savannah at the creek had been a far cry from the one who'd been surprised earlier by my being at her safe place.

But then we got back from dinner.

And then she showered.

...And all bets were off.

How in the hell was I going to sleep in a bed next to her, after she'd showered and smelled like that body wash she'd been using for years? The one that smelled like the beach?

Even her shampoo was coconut scented.

And her lotion.

Shit, I was so screwed.

I ignored my libido when she came out of the bathroom and she passed the shower off to me.

"Should be hot water left. I wasn't in there that long."

I knew this water heater, and I knew just how long she'd been in the shower.

There wouldn't be any hot water left, but I wasn't complaining. I needed a hot shower like I needed a slap in the face.

A cold shower could hopefully cure what currently ailed me—a reminder of my need for Savannah.

Earlier, out at the creek before Savannah joined me, I'd been thinking about that summer we'd found the little thinking spot.

I remembered talking about the guy Savannah had recently dumped.

And yes, *she* dumped *him*, and I remember being so damn proud of her because he'd been a tool. She wasn't happy with him, and he was an ass to anyone he wasn't friends with. I'd been afraid she'd stick it out with him because they'd only been dating for a couple of weeks.

He'd asked her out after she never showed up to prom.

I never understood why she told him yes, but she did.

So when she dumped him after seeing the error in her ways, I hugged her and told her she was too good for him.

I could remember her going silent then, and I know I didn't think anything of it then, and maybe it was me projecting now, but I thought maybe...

It had something to do with me?

Yeah. Absolute projecting right now.

I had to get to the bottom of these feelings.

I had to bring them up to Savannah.

I had to stop acting like a damn child and just say it.

I took the fastest cold shower of my life, my intentions high—I was going to get out there, and we were going to hash out the last three years.

It was one thing to be a fifteen year old kid who didn't think he could possibly like-like his best friend.

It was another thing to be twenty-six and playing the "does she like me, does she not like me" game.

I knew Savannah as well as I knew myself.

What the hell was stopping me from telling her I loved her?

Shower complete, I dried off just as quickly and threw on the clean sweatpants and t-shirt I had for bed. Rubbing on my deodorant, I thought about what I wanted to say and how I wanted to say it.

I knew that if I straight out told her, *Look, I think that you have feelings for me and that's why you wouldn't take me to the airport,* she'd clam up.

If I said, *I want to talk about your twenty-first birthday,* she'd get flustered and continue to deny, deny, deny.

I knew that if I were to do anything, I was going to have to come at it from a "me" angle. My thoughts. My feelings. My desires.

My fears. My transgressions.

I said no to Bella because she's not you.

That.

I said no to Bella because she wasn't Savannah.

She'd have questions. She likely wouldn't believe anything right away, but if I started with that, and then told her everything else, surely she'd believe it.

Right?

Yes.

Plan in place, I stepped out of the bathroom.

The cabin was quiet but for the fire going in the fireplace. Stepping toward the bed, I saw that Savannah was in it—and fast asleep.

Like a deflated balloon, everything in me dropped.

I was really working on the impulsive angle and now knowing the conversation wouldn't be had until at least morning...

Well, shit.

But I also wasn't about to wake her up.

Instead, I moved to the unoccupied side of the bed and slipped under the covers. Laying on my back, I looked over to my left, where Savannah lay on her side, her back to me.

Just like old times.

I imagined rolling up to her and being the big spoon to her little one. The more the thought took hold in my head, the higher my desire grew. Trying to fall asleep with a boner wasn't going to do me any favors, so I forced the train of thought off and rolled to my side, away from her.

I stared at the fire for what felt like hours, but eventually dozed to sleep.

* * *

"You're my number one. Always will be," I told her, my hand on her cheek as she looked up at me. Those brown eyes that I've loved for years, the ones that spoke so many truths.

She was in my bed.

I knew that it was a bad idea, sleeping with her. We were both a little bit wasted from celebrating her twenty-first but those eyes...

They told me she was with this, one-hundred percent.

"You're my number one, too," Savannah whispered, her words strong and sure. Her fingers played with the belt loops of my jeans, but neither of us was rushing anything. I wanted to taste every inch of her, and to start, I wanted her mouth.

I wanted to devour and learn her.

Swallow her moans and let my hands wander as her mouth played against mine, telling me without words she wanted me as much as I wanted her.

"I'm going to kiss you now."

Her smile was wide. "I was hoping you would."

But as my lips dropped to hers, the woman in front of me changed.

No longer was it Savannah, but it was Bella.

I tried to pull back before my lips landed, but Bella's hands were on my head, forcing me to her.

Before I could stop it, the words were out again.

"You're my number one."

I woke suddenly, confused at the course of my dream.

But just as I started to get my bearings, I heard the soft sound coming from behind me.

"You're my number one."

It was my voice, followed by...

"That's the sweetest thing anyone has ever told me."

And that was Bella's voice.

Then it was silent for a brief moment, before, "You're my number one," played again.

Suddenly, the timing of Savannah's need to get away made sense.

I remembered that day on the show, and knew that it was when I was in the top four. It had to have been the most recent episode.

"That's the—" Silence. Maybe even a sniffle. "You're my number one."

Shit. Was she crying?

I didn't know what to do.

For all my bravado earlier before bed, I was suddenly at a loss for words, and I knew that if I told Savannah I was awake, she'd freak out.

But I also couldn't keep hearing the words that were once only for Savannah, being told to Bella in a moment of weakness.

A moment where I was no longer seeing Bella, but imagining Savannah.

A moment that I realized now, maybe hurt my best friend...

I knew once I got that far in the show, when the feelings for Savannah didn't go away but instead grew by the day, that I should have walked.

But I didn't.

Part of me kept holding out, *hoping* for, things to change. For me to realize Savannah was my best friend and that was all she would be. That it was all *she* wanted it to be.

I was beginning to realize that wasn't the case.

And if I heard my voice one more time, I was going to lose it.

So, I closed my eyes again and slowly fell from my side to my back, as if rearranging in sleep. I could feel Savannah freeze beside me—I could even hear that she held her breath.

When I didn't make another move other than a heavy sigh, I heard what sounded like her putting her phone under her pillow, then trying to settle in for sleep once again.

If Savannah had the same feelings I had...why did she push me away when we had the opportunity to make something more of our friendship?

What little sleep I'd already gotten tonight was going to be it, because I knew without a doubt my mind would be rolling with thoughts of Savannah for the rest of the night.

CHAPTER SEVEN

SAVANNAH

My pillow was moving.

As I slowly woke up, I also realized my pillow was warm.

And hard.

And my hand wasn't grasping the fitted sheet, but the white t-shirt Ryan wore.

Oh, shit.

In all the years we'd slept in the same bed, this scenario had never happened before.

Well. That one time. After we fuc— made lo— had sex. We woke up like this then too.

But now was not the time.

No, not the time at all.

I tried to move off of his chest slowly, but...

"Why did you need Colorado?"

His voice was low and sexy, but not sleepy.

Ryan didn't hold me to him; he let me move away.

But I knew he wasn't going to drop the conversation. It was in the tone of his words. He was settled for a conversation, no matter how difficult it would be for me.

And it was going to be difficult. I needed to figure out my angle.

"I need coffee for this conversation. And to brush my teeth," I managed to say, slightly embarrassed by my sleep-thickened voice.

Before I could climb out of bed, his hand shot out and he grabbed my forearm. "No."

Shocked at his refusal, I finally looked, taking all of him in.

His face looked tired. His jawline showcased a deeper scruff than yesterday. His white t-shirt looked like I'd been holding on for dear life for a lot longer than a few minutes.

And his eyes...

They looked determined.

"I know you, Savannah. I know damn well you're going to step away and your brain is going to move a million miles a minute, and then once you've had your coffee and you've started your day, you'll come up with a hundred new excuses why we can't have this conversation. I let it go yesterday. I'm not letting it go today. So settle in." His words were serious, but that last bit...

It was jovial in tone and the side of his mouth quirked up.

"I..."

Didn't know what to say, that was what.

"Just talk to me, Sav. What happened? We used to talk about everything, and if that night truly meant nothing, if you truly thought it was a mistake, it would not have affected our friendship," he said, going straight for the jugular.

My face, I was sure, was ten shades of red, and the center of my chest itched in a way I knew was not going to go away.

"Please let me go," I whispered, now avoiding his eyes.

Instead, I locked my eyes on the center of his shirt, focusing on the rise and fall of his chest.

"Savannah," he pleaded, his own voice low, but he did as I asked and released my arm.

I shot up off the bed. "I just..." I turned away and started for the bathroom. "Just give me a minute, please."

Once again, I found myself hiding in the bathroom. This morning though, I sat on the floor with my knees up to my chest and my forehead resting on them, as I squeezed my eyes shut and counted to one hundred. My body rocked with each beat of my heart, but every time I noticed the gentle sway, I forced my attention back to the numbers.

At one hundred, I began counting down backward, slowly and in time with my inhales.

Outside the bathroom door, I could hear as Ryan moved around the cabin. Again, I tried not to focus on those noises and back internally, but it was no use.

My mind craved to find him.

Knowing there was nowhere for me to go but out there to confront every thought I'd had over the last three years, I stood and brushed my teeth, staring at my reflection.

Mentally going over everything I could say, and everything he could respond with.

Of course, my initial thoughts on how he would react were negative.

He'd laugh.

He'd tell me I was crazy.

That I was just his friend.

That nothing changed for him.

But then my therapist's words filtered in: *what negative thinking pattern is this?*

Jumping to conclusions.

Making negative assumptions.

Your feelings are legitimate.

My feelings.

Were.

Legitimate.

And it was okay if they weren't the same feelings Ryan had, but I couldn't keep on this spiral of self-hate all because I was worried about what he was thinking.

Spitting out the toothpaste foam in my mouth, I wiped my lips and chin with the back of my hand and stared hard.

"You've got this," I whispered to my reflection. "Own your feelings. They're legitimate."

I took a deep breath and nodded a couple more times.

My head was going to fall off with all the nodding, but sometimes you just needed some self-affirmation.

For the first time since I realized I was going to be in close confines with my best friend, slash the man I was pretty sure I was in love with, slash the man I was pretty sure I couldn't have—at least, until learning that he told Bella no (just what the hell did that mean?)—I had a sense of ease.

I felt powerful in my feelings.

You're going to open the door and that feeling will evaporate.

I really hated that fucking devil on my shoulder.

Ignoring it, I pulled open the door and immediately found Ryan standing at the counter. He still wore the sweatpants and t-shirt he went to bed in, which I supposed, unless he were to change in the open bedroom area, he'd have to be in.

His clothes weren't tight, but they also weren't loose, so

I could make out the muscles of his upper back working as he moved. I let my eyes drop to his ass.

He had a nice ass.

Definitely an athlete's ass. Round and firm and filled his sweatpants.

I swallowed hard, feeling slightly guilty at watching him. But then again, it wasn't like he didn't know I was here.

He had to have heard the bathroom door open.

He knew I was watching, but he let me have my time.

Pulling my shoulders back, I took a deep breath and answered his first question, my eyes focused on the center of his back.

"I came to Colorado because I needed a hard reset after watching you tell a beautiful woman the very words you've told me since I was eleven years old." Ryan's upper body stiffened. "I needed out of the apartment that held memories of you." He flipped off the hot plate and turned, but I kept my eyes plastered to the center of his chest. "I needed away from the complex that you lived just down the hall. I needed to not see Mitch and be reminded that you weren't there and instead, were with another woman."

Ryan moved now, coming near, and it took all of me to not take a step back.

To hold firm in my spot.

My heart was racing and I felt like I couldn't get in enough oxygen, but I had to do this. I had to finish this.

I had to get it all out.

"I didn't have an obligation," I admitted, still avoiding his face even though he now stood two feet in front of me. "I just couldn't pretend to be happy for you when I was slowly dying inside."

I swallowed hard before answering the next of his questions—one of the things I learned early on in my therapy was I had hyperthymesia. An extremely detailed autobiographical memory. "I hesitated in applying at O'Gallagher's because I was still reeling from my twenty-first birthday and I was having a hard time being around you. It was easy to pretend everything was fine from a distance, but knowing that I'd be spending even more time with you... It was difficult for me. And then you and Mitch moved into the same complex I'd moved into after college...and it was almost too much."

Finally, I dared myself to move my focal point and blinked, opening my eyes so they landed on his face.

A face that seemed closed off of any emotion. His eyes were focused on my face. His mouth was relaxed.

But nothing gave way to what he was feeling.

"Ryan, you are my one constant in life. Have been for as long as I remember. I had two parents who were supposed to love and support me, but only one seemed to sign on for that job. The other, no matter how hard I tried, I continuously disappointed. Even now, I'm a disappointment to her. I'm learning that that's on her, that I shouldn't own those feelings. But the only other person who has been in my life for longer than a few years is you, and it would absolutely kill me to lose your friendship.

"I want to be able to talk to you when things go bad," I continued, even though tears began to threaten. "I want to be able to support you in everything that you do. But I want to be able to support you and not feel like I'm drowning, which is why I was such a terrible friend when you left. I was drowning. And then with that last episode with Bella...I felt like I was being swept away by the current. I don't know how to be your friend right now. Not when you're moving on, and I'm still stuck in my head, on July twenty-first."

I swallowed hard and forced myself to stand still, to not retreat.

"I want to be happy for you when you find the woman of your dreams," my voice cracked but I held on, keeping my eyes trained on his. When his mouth parted to speak, I kept going. "I want to watch you get married and have babies, and raise them to be the most perfect little humans. I want to be happy being Aunt Savvy. And I know that I'll get there. I just have to get all of these feelings off my chest. I can't keep them bottled up. If there's one night I regret, it's my birthday. For three years, I haven't been able to let it go, and in doing so, I've single-handedly strained our friendship. And I'm sorry. I'm a terrible friend."

I shook my head, proud that I owned my feelings but sad that I had to put them to voice. Sad that they would likely firmly change the course of our friendship.

All I had left were my apologies. So I whispered them again. "I'm so sorry."

CHAPTER EIGHT

RYAN

My hands itched to take her face and make her look at me. Make her understand what she meant to me.

Her words drove daggers into my heart.

There was a real pain in the center of my chest, listening to her tell me how she wanted me to be happy, and how she wanted to be happy when I found my wife, and have my kids, and lived my life.

As if she were going to be a bystander.

If I couldn't hold her face and make her focus on me, then I wanted to hold her hand, but even that seemed to be too many steps forward. I ought to take this at her pace.

But I'd *been* taking it at her pace and because of that, I enabled any and all negative self-talk she had.

Because of my bruised ego, I let her walk away. I let her put space between us.

It was time to fix that.

"Do you know the first thing I noticed about you?" I asked softly, my eyes locked on hers.

When she shook her head, I continued, "Your smile. You'd just moved basically across the country, but you were happy doing your thing. You were drawing on the driveway, smiling to yourself, absolutely content with yourself and the life you had. Where did she go? Where is that Savannah?"

She opened her mouth, but quickly closed it, averting her eyes at the same time. This time, I allowed myself to guide my hand to her face, and bring her attention back to me. "I'll tell you where. She gets tucked away until you're comfortable. Until everything around you is in the boxes and spaces that make you feel safe. Whenever your world started to crash around you, I knew that I could bring you back to her. I knew that I could bring my Savannah back. It gives a man, or even a boy back then, a sense of pride, to know he can do that for someone. It became my one goal in life. Make Savannah smile. Bring the light to her eyes. And for a long damn time, I was successful. But I made one giant mistake."

Savannah shook her head. "No, you didn't."

"I did." I brought my other hand up so I was framing her face. "That morning, I was riding a high." I didn't need to specify the morning. She knew. "And then you looked over at me and freaked. Told me it had been a mistake, that we'd been too drunk. But Savannah, I was with you one hundred percent that night. And if the blush on your cheeks is any indication, you remember as much of that night as I do.

"That night had been a long time coming. Drinking was an excuse. It was too dumb to try and broach the subject without an excuse, and when I brought you back to my place and kissed you, and you whispered that you wanted me..." I shook my head lightly, "It was like my entire world finally connected. The puzzle pieces that were there, finally connected. Savannah Slate, I have loved you since I was ten years old."

Her brown eyes widened and her mouth dropped.

When she brought her hands up to my wrists, I pushed on. "So that morning... After the best night of my life, you pushing away... God, Savannah, it was an ego thing. And I let you stay away because I was licking my own wounds, and then when we finally started to hang out again and you pretended like everything was cool, well, it killed me but I followed your lead.

"Ask me why I don't drink," I added, changing the subject abruptly.

Savannah swallowed hard before whispering the question that was seemingly left-field. "Why don't you drink, Ryan?"

"Because without fail, I get drunk and I think of you. I remember that night. I remember you in my arms. I remember your taste, your body, your moans. Ask me why I wasn't pissed at Mitch for signing me up for the show."

Her voice still soft and unsure, she did as I asked. "Why weren't you angry with him?"

"Because that week at the bar, you wouldn't look at me but flirted with five different guys, including Jake." Jake was another bartender that we worked with. One who happened to be happily married, but it had still stung. "You could work with him and be happy, but you couldn't work with me and be happy." I lowered my voice, the emotion stirring in my heart and gut making it increasingly harder to get the words out. "Ask me—"

"Why did you tell Bella no?" Savannah interrupted. Rather than be annoyed that she broke my train, I was so damn proud of her for finding her voice.

"Because Bella isn't you."

"But you told her—"

"I know what I told her. I heard you replaying the clip last night," I confessed. That damn clip was the reason we were having this conversation.

She gasped lightly but I shook my head.

"I don't know how to prove it to you, but Savannah, I was thinking of you. I know that's a bullshit answer, and it makes me look like an ass, but I was trying to feel something for her. The further along I got in the show, the more I'd dream of you. The more I'd see you. If anything, being in that environment showed me that it's you that I want. That I crave. That I need. But I did it because I thought that we were on different wave lengths. We didn't want the same thing.

"Savannah, if you tell me that the most we can ever be is friends, now with everything out there, I will respect that. I will hate it, but I will respect it." I shook my head slightly, "But I don't think I can be a good friend, watching you marry the man of *your* dreams, because you are the woman of *mine*. I can't be happy watching you have babies, because I want you to have *my* babies. So I'm pretty sure that makes *me* the terrible friend."

Her mouth worked but words didn't come out. She did, however, drop her hands from my wrists and I felt that loss as if she were stepping miles away.

Finally, she said, "This is a lot to process. I... I can't... I need..."

"I understand." I let go of her face, even though my gut was yelling at me to kiss her and make her understand. Get her on the same page.

But I couldn't do that to her.

I could see the panic in her eyes, even though I told her essentially what she'd told me. It was more than clear that she was supposed to be mine, and I was supposed to be hers, but those damn fears of hers...

Hell, I'd be lucky if she even *heard* half of what I said, with the way her anxieties tended to block things.

Before I could come up with anything that I *could* do, the factory-installed ringing on my phone broke through the thick silence.

"Saved by the bell," Savannah tried to joke, but it was forced. Just like my answering smile.

I turned to pick up my phone from the counter, seeing the saved number pop up.

It was the show.

"I've got to take this," I apologized but she just shook her head and stepped away, back toward the bed.

"Hello?" I answered, leaning back into the counter but watching Savannah move. She went to her backpack and pulled out clothes, tossing them on the end of the bed.

"Hey, Ryan. This is Tony. We've had to make some adjustments to the finale." Savannah rezipped her backpack and picked up her clothes, avoiding looking in my direction as she made her way back to the bathroom. I heard the door click and soon after, the shower turned on. "We're told we have to shut down production because of this virus. All the companies are doing it, and we're a day behind them. So, what we're going to do is a live stream in place of the finale. We'd prefer it if you did it with Bella, but with California on the verge of public lock down—and let's be honest, New York is probably only a day or two behind California—she said she won't travel to you. There may be necessary quarantining for you too, if you travel out of California, which would mean you wouldn't be able to do it with her anyway. It's just a fucking mess."

Tony wasn't the most eloquent with his words. How he managed to produce so many of these dating shows was beyond me.

"The final episode is airing on Monday, and we want to go live with you and Bella directly afterward. We'll be sending you specifics here shortly, but if you need to increase your internet package, you need to do it before then. Oh, and I'll be sending you over the last show, so you can prepare for the finale. We'll be going live before the show airs in California."

"Sounds good," I mumbled, my eyes still fixed on the bathroom door.

"You can still fix how you ended the show."

Yeah. Not happening. "Sounds good," I repeated, knowing that nothing I said would matter to him.

Rumor had it, he tried the same thing on an earlier show he produced, one with one of the regulars at O'Gallagher's, Caleb Prescott, who also happened to coach the local NHL team.

Caleb's show, *Beauty*, was like *The Rose*, but instead of regular—or, mostly regular, because Bella was an actress—people, the bachelor or bachelorette was an athlete. It only aired for three seasons and none of the on-show pairings worked out (Caleb and his wife were an odd sort of exception, because Sydney didn't win, but Caleb didn't exactly vote her off either), but Tony immediately put together *The Rose* afterward, and in seventeen years, became the top rated dating show.

Seventeen years, thirty-four pairings from two seasons a year, ten marriages, eight kids, and now, thanks to me, one "no."

"Bella is open to working things out," Tony continued pushing.

"I've got to go, Tony. Thank you. I look forward to your email and talking on Monday." Before he could go on even more, I ended the phone call, and tossed the device on the counter, where it slid a good two feet.

Turning to my breakfast, I quickly ate my now cold eggs, but I couldn't stop hearing Savannah's words.

How they went from quiet and unsure, to strong and needing to know.

Then, back to that unsure, unsettled tone again.

I gave her my words.

I gave her my feelings.

I didn't know what else I could do, other than give her time.

And hope like hell that she'd trust me.

Once my eggs were done, I went to the fireplace and started a new fire. The cabin was starting to get chilled and looking out the window, I realized it was because it had started to snow.

Unsure what to do next—for the last six weeks, this was what I'd been doing too; living in solitude with nothing but my thoughts—I stared out the window by the rocking chair, my arms crossed, waiting for Savannah to emerge from the bathroom, as I watched the white flutter to the ground, slowly building.

In a one room cabin like this one, the only place to hide was the bathroom, and hiding was exactly what she was doing.

Eventually while staring out the window, my gaze

glossed over and I was no longer watching the steady snow fall, but remember the early morning hours, when Savannah slept beside me and I watched her.

When she rolled to her back for a moment, before rolling into my side.

When she placed her head on my chest and sighed softly through slightly parted lips.

Remembering the sound had my dick swelling again, just as it had much earlier this morning. All I'd wanted to do was wrap her in my arms, hold her tight, get as close to her as I could.

But that wasn't what friends did.

What would my future look like without Savannah in it? I wondered. If the words we just shared fully and finally scared her away, how would my days look?

No longer would I have those moments that I looked forward to. At least, not every day. Knowing her, she'd probably quit O'Gallagher's. Maybe even find a new apartment.

Us living in the same complex—again—was a little bit coincidental. It was near the light rail which worked for both Mitch and I, and the complex had a two-bedroom available when our other choice wouldn't for a few more weeks after when we'd needed it.

For the longest time, I thought Savannah and I ended up in the same places because we were meant to be with one another.

Even if not romantically, she was my person.

My mom once told me that soulmates didn't have to be romantic; you could have a soulmate that was a friend.

But thinking back to that conversation, back to when I

sat on the couch in my parent's living room when I was eighteen, getting ready to move away for college, and telling my mom that I feared losing Savannah's friendship...

She held my hand and smiled at me, her voice soft, telling me that the soul knew what it wanted, and we were drawn to certain people. *"Your soulmate can very well be a very best friend. It doesn't have to be someone that you fall in romantic love with. You two were drawn together since the first moment you met. Your friendship was meant to be and can survive anything. Although...never mind."*

My mom knew that I loved my best friend. I now didn't have a doubt in my head that that was the direction her thoughts were going.

"What do you mean, you haven't talked to Savannah this week?" My mother scolded me on the phone when asking about side dishes for Thanksgiving, two years ago. "You live right down the hall! You work together! Please tell me you didn't do something stupid to hurt her."

"I haven't done anything stupid, mother. We just have had crazy different schedules." Even I knew the excuse was weak.

"Well, you talk to that girl, and ask her if she wants green beans or asparagus. 'Haven't talked to her'," she scoffed silently. "You haven't not talked to her hardly ever in your lives. Don't think you're too grown for a good ass whoppin' if you hurt Savannah."

I didn't doubt it but again, "I didn't hurt her, mom." At least, I didn't think so.

If anyone hurt anybody, it was Savannah who hurt me. I was at least grateful she was kind of talking to me these days.

The bathroom door opened and I turned toward the

woman who held my thoughts.

Savannah walked out, holding her pajamas to her chest as her wet brown hair fell over a shoulder. She never was one for a lot of makeup, but now, fully fresh faced, she reminded me so much of the young girl she once was.

She'd always been a pretty girl, but my God, she grew up to be a beautiful woman. She constantly took my breath away, even when I was struggling to figure out how to mend our bent pieces.

"It's snowing." Captain Obvious, that was me.

She tipped her head slightly to look around me, and I watched her brows raise. "Shit. It's *really* snowing."

Turning, I looked to see what she saw, and sure enough, sometime in the last however many minutes, the sky truly opened up. What little snow I had watched a bit ago, was now coming down harder, thicker. I couldn't see our cars out the window, and they were only a few feet away.

I heard Savannah sigh, turning back to her as she deposited her clothes on the bed and picked up her phone from under her pillow. She punched things onto the screen, and then groaned aloud. "Well, shoot," she mumbled, and I stepped closer, wanting to see what she was seeing.

"What's up?"

"Blizzard warning." Her words were still mumbled as she moved through her screen. "And the radar looks bad." Finally, she turned the phone to me and sure enough, the radar made it look like it was going to be snowing for a good while.

"Looks like we're stuck. You didn't plan on going anywhere today anyway, did you?"

She shook her head but looked disappointed. "I have a

book I can read."

"Or..." I paused, waiting for her to connect those brown beauties on my eyes, "we can watch a movie? Like old times?" It was my peace offering, to try and get past that intense moment, and find ourselves again.

"Ryan. I can't..." She sighed heavily and looking at her face, I realized she was tired. Not physically, but mentally. Or, more so, emotionally spent. "After what was just said, there is no, 'like old times'." She held her hands out in front of her like two giant stop signs. "I don't know what to think with you, and I don't know what parts of my memories are true or false. I need space." I could hear the anxiety starting to grow in her words, and she capitalized it with her final jab, "And now I'm stuck here with you." She quickly turned away from me, and I knew without a doubt she was on the verge of crying.

And, while it made me a shit friend, I wanted to push.

Even though she was clearly hurting, I wanted to get past this wall that she kept creating between us.

Because I was hurting too; I just wasn't as visible about it.

"You have the best memory of anyone that I know, Savannah. Whatever you remember, the actual events and words, is likely true. The falseness would be whatever bullshit your mind chooses to filter in." Harsh, but I couldn't keep handling her with kid gloves.

Savannah was a grown woman who, thirty minutes ago, seemed to own her feelings but now, whiplash central, and she was pulling away.

A-fucking-gain.

She swung back toward me, her arm shooting out to

point a finger at me, no doubt pissed at me and my choice of words. "Any bullshit is from years of rejection."

She did not just clump me in with her mother.

I couldn't stop the anger from my voice if I tried. "I have *never* rejected you!"

"Didn't you?" She stepped closer and poked me in the chest. "Didn't you let me walk away?"

"Savannah, what the hell was I supposed to do? I couldn't get a word in edgewise! You were on a mission to leave my apartment and refused to let me talk."

"You had a moment. When you told me I was your 'number one. Always will be.'" She spat the words back to me, and the disdain was thick in her voice.

"It was the only way I knew how to tell you I loved you. Because I knew damn well the words themselves wouldn't be taken well."

"You don't let someone you love walk away."

"You sure as fuck do when you realize your feelings are one sided. When everything your mind and heart had been building up came crashing down because *you* said it was a mistake. Savannah, I've made a lot of mistakes in my life, but making love to you is not, and could not ever be, one of them."

Apparently, those words were too real for her, because she shook her head again. Her go-to move when things weren't going the way she needed them to go for her sanity. Well, what about mine?

"I don't want to do this right now," she announced.

"Too fucking bad. We're doing it now. You have nowhere to go. You can't see a foot in front of you outside. We're stuck here. And if anything, this conversation is three years too late. Now is the *perfect* time."

She screwed up her lips and shook her head, before turning away from me, trying to shut me out in the only way she knew how.

"Your mother may let you close up and shut her out, but that's because she's a piece of shit."

I half expected her to call *me* a piece of shit because that was basically what I did when she walked away from me three years ago—let her close up and shut me out. But I knew better than to expect her to say anything.

Savannah was in shut down mode.

I'd be lucky if she spoke to me at all the rest of the day.

Hell, I'd be lucky if she spoke to me by the end of the weekend.

This was what she was best at.

It was her version of protecting herself, to hell with whoever she hurt along the way.

The thing was, this had never truly hurt anyone other than herself in the past. She shut her mom out, but her mom gave two shits.

Now, she was shutting me out, and this felt like more than the last time.

I had a terrible feeling that there was a chance I would truly lose my friend after this weekend.

But I couldn't live with myself if I didn't give her all of my truths.

Like her therapist told her again and again, and Savannah reported back to me, feelings are valid.

My feelings were valid.

And yes, her feelings were valid too, but sometimes her damn mind liked to twist things.

Knowing that anything that I said now would be futile, I let her have her silence.

For now.

CHAPTER NINE

SAVANNAH

I knew shutting him out was childish.

I knew that the adult thing to do was to talk to him.

But I was terrified.

Petrified, even.

I was even slightly embarrassed.

He'd caught me watching the show replay last night. When he turned over in his sleep, he hadn't really been sleeping.

And I was the fool who was caught pining over something she couldn't have.

But can't you?

This was a different voice than the one that I often called the devil. The devil was the negative thoughts that played over and over. My anxiety dealt with a lot of untruths.

Rarely did it deal with potential.

I didn't know what to do with those words.

However, I let them simmer in the back of my mind as I read a new book on my Kindle app, from one of my favorite authors. I'd started the book on the plane, and was now to the black moment—the moment in a romance where either an outside force tried to tear the couple apart, or as was the case in this book, when the hero did something stupid to drive the heroine away.

Again, the words repeated in my head: *But can't you?*

Why couldn't I have Ryan? Why couldn't I believe what he told me? For the first half of my life, I believed every word he said.

He was my savior.

My rock.

And never once lied to me.

The negative thought pattern started to try and push through, trying to convince me that there couldn't be something there, but I mentally knocked it back before full sentences could form in my mind. I knew where the negative thoughts were going, and I wanted nothing to do with them.

Why couldn't I believe that he'd loved me since we were young?

I mean...

I cared about him.

So deeply.

To the point where I often pictured him as the hero in my books, and I was the heroine, and it wasn't hard to believe the confessions of love when I read a love story as if it were us in the pages of the book. I didn't know that my feelings for Ryan were love, but putting us in my stories...

I could relate to the heroines.

I was curled up at the top of the bed, my knees drawn up as I held my phone by my thighs, and I peeked my eyes toward where Ryan sat at the small kitchen table. He had Bluetooth ear pods in and watched his phone. I wondered briefly if it was a movie, like he'd invited me to do with him, but then his face made an expression of thought.

Not an expression I'd expect if he were watching the

latest Christian Bale film.

When he shifted in the chair, I immediately brought my eyes back to my book and tried to concentrate but now, after I'd let my mind wander, I knew it was a worthless task.

The words were beginning to swim and cause a headache.

Putting my phone down, I uncurled from myself and walked over to the kitchen, trying to keep my focus and attention ahead of me, but still being very attuned to Ryan in the chair.

I wanted him to turn and ask me what I was up to.

But when he didn't, I couldn't blame him.

I grabbed an apple and quickly cleaned it in the sink, and my mind wandered to a silly TikTok I'd watched at the airport yesterday.

Girls kissing their best guy friends.

While watching it, I couldn't help but wonder what Ryan's reaction would be—because while I'd been fighting my feelings for him tooth and nail, my subconscious clearly tried drawing me back to him again and again—and now, while my mind was a full mess after our fight, I couldn't help but think about his words.

The ones of love.

In the videos, most reactions had been positive, and I remember thinking that they had to be set up. Not truthful. Those people were so dating.

I took a giant bite from my apple, looking out the window above the sink. We were definitely snowed in, and if I were to, I don't know, decide to do this silly stupid thing that all the young kids were doing, and Ryan rejected the advance...

You really think he's going to reject you kissing him?

I wasn't sure when the devil of negativity was traded for this positive thought pattern, but...

I kind of liked it.

However, just the thought of walking over to him and surprising him, putting my lips on his...

My heart began to race.

My stomach churned in panic.

"I have loved you since I was ten years old."

I found that I wanted to believe his words.

...that maybe even, I *did* believe his words.

A warm feeling rushed through me at the thought of possibility.

Of potential.

Of *more*.

I was going to do it.

I let that declaration fuel my steps across the room and to where he sat.

And when my heart pounded harder, so hard it felt like it was going to come right out of my chest, I pushed through.

I didn't even look to see what he was watching. Didn't try to get his attention.

Instead, I reached around his face and turned his chin toward me. His eyes moved to mine and his lips parted, but before he could say something, and before I could lose my nerve, I dropped my mouth to his, pressing my lips to his in a kiss that was so innocent. Far more innocent than I was sure his kisses with Bella ever were.

However, just as that Bella jab entered my thoughts, I heard Ryan's phone drop to the table and his hands were on my ass. He flexed his fingers before he turned himself in the chair, and guided me to his lap.

I pulled my mouth away but his mouth followed mine and soon, the kiss wasn't so innocent.

Not when his tongue brushed against my lips, asking for permission to take the kiss further.

Willingly, I opened my mouth to his advances and the moment our tongues brushed, my fingers pressed into his cheek before dropping to his shoulder.

This wasn't a man who maybe kind of sort of felt something for his best friend.

This kiss was from a man who, at the very least, was attracted to the woman in his lap—even if she maybe ran hot and cold and gave major whiplash over the last twenty-four hours.

Curiosity won out, and I moved from sitting sideways, to straddling his lap.

The second that my core came in contact with the hard ridge of his erection, we both gasped. Rather than the kiss stopping though, Ryan took it deeper.

I wanted his hands on my skin.

I wanted *my* hands on *his* skin.

Frantically, I dropped my arms to try and work his shirt up and off, but that seemed to be the magic button to get Ryan to snap back to present.

"Savannah." My name was said on a groan, and when I tried to push through and kept working on his shirt, he moved his hands from my ass to cover my hands, effectively halting my movements. "Savannah."

My breathing was labored and through parted lips. I fisted my hands in the material of his shirt, but was growing nervous.

Licking my lips, I fought to maintain eye contact.

"What...what is this?" His question was soft, but nothing changed—he was still hard and his pupils were still dilated.

"I, um." I swallowed hard. "I..."

I couldn't get the words out. On one hand, the "mistake" angle was on the tip of my tongue, but on the other, that Positive Polly who made her voice known this afternoon was urging me to stay. To fight for what I wanted.

Ryan didn't force words from me, and the longer our eyes stayed locked, the more my nerves settled and the stronger I felt.

This man was aroused.

He was attracted to me.

It didn't matter than I pushed and fought; he was still here for me.

And he wasn't pushing me away.

If anything, he was holding me secure in his lap.

"I've been stupid," I whispered, the moment the words entered my mind. For once, I didn't think about what I was going to say before I said them.

For the majority of my life, every word out of my mouth had been thought over to death, and—like Ryan said—filtered with negativity.

This speaking before thinking was new, but I was starting to think it could be freeing.

"I've let my fears put a huge wall between us, when you've never done anything to truly deserve it."

"Savannah—"

I shook my head and wiggled one hand from his, and put it on the side of his neck, my thumb resting on his jawline. "What would life have been like if I didn't run scared?" I wondered aloud.

This time, Ryan shook his head before surprising me—keeping his eyes on mine, he turned his in toward my hand and kissed my thumb. "Don't do that. You can't do the what if game."

He sounded like my therapist. "Who taught you that? Your mom?" I asked with a small smile.

His mom was one of the most wonderful women I've ever known.

Ryan smiled against my thumb before turning his face back to mine. "She's a very smart woman, but I think it was actually you, after your mom left. From your therapist."

"Makes sense." I let my hand drop from his neck but rather than just land in my lap, Ryan took it in his and squeezed.

"Can I watch something with you?" His question was paired with an unsure look on his features, and my go-to response was to freeze.

For my walls to go back up.

And of course, he sensed that.

"I want to explain some things to you," he said, squeezing my hand again and holding it tight, "and I don't want you to doubt my actions or things that I say. Today, tomorrow, in the future. And I think I have a way to show you you've been the one on my mind. I was watching last week's episode, and I think you maybe missed some things."

I wanted to trust my gut.

And my gut was telling me that I've trusted Ryan this many years; I could continue to trust him now. So I nodded, hoping that whatever he would show me wouldn't hurt the fragile pieces of my heart that were only now starting to mend.

CHAPTER TEN

RYAN

"Maybe on the bed. Just...more comfortable." Honestly, she could sit on my lap all night, but I also knew that the longer she sat here, the more uncomfortable—needy—I was getting.

And as badly as my cock wanted it, I was *not* taking Savannah tonight.

"Oh, okay." For the first time since she took rein of her feelings, she dropped her eyes.

"None of that, Sav," I said softly, and she brought her eyes back up and smiled slightly. "I just want to stretch out. And thought it would be easier to watch and explain over there."

An image of the two of us in bed, sans clothes, flashed across my mind, and my cock twitched in anticipation.

Okay, so maybe *not* the best course of action, but I'd already committed, so I was following through.

With a hand in hers and my other on her hip, I guided Savannah off me and when I stood after dropping her hand, I couldn't help but grimace at the tightness of my lap. I didn't miss when Savannah lowered her eyes and the fast blush that decorated her cheeks, before she turned away, leading the way to the bed.

Yeah.

Sweatpants weren't the most ideal in my current situation.

Nothing I could do about it now.

I grabbed my phone from the table and followed behind her.

Savannah settled on the left side of the bed, adjusting her pillow so it supported her back as she sat against the headboard. I moved to my side and took up residence beside her, bringing my knee up to try and relieve some of the tent action happening because of my erection.

With my phone in hand, I reopened the video I'd been studying before Savannah surprised the hell out of me.

I couldn't believe she kissed me!

Hell, I'd be thinking about that kiss for the rest of my life.

"If I know you at all," I started to say, scrolling through the episode, "you shut everything off after I told Bella...after what I said."

Savannah shifted but didn't answer.

"Which means you missed something. Something I didn't realize would be put in the show, but I guess it's probably a good marketing piece." I was a little pissed at being a ploy for ratings, but I also was grateful that they caught it *and* put it in the final cut.

I moved the streaming cursor to just after the-day-that-shall-not-be-named, when the show cut to a scene where the camera was focused on a closed door, but my voice could be heard.

"You ready?" I looked down at her and while her eyes were fixed on my phone, she nodded.

"As ready as I'll ever be."

I pressed the triangle in the middle of the screen and moved the phone so it was more between us, and held down the volume button to turn it all the way up.

The sound of a ringing phone was cut off by a muffled, "Hello?"

"How is she?" My voice carried through the closed door. I was speaking low to try and not be overheard, but in a place that was set up with microphones in every corner, it was almost pointless.

There wasn't any sound for a pause, other than what sounded like me rearranging my stance, leaving the watcher to assume I was standing behind the door.

"She's...good."

"That's Mitch's voice." Savannah's tone was confused and I glanced at her to see her brows furrowed.

"Shh."

"I just... I can't..." It was clear I was frustrated. "Fuck, I can't stop thinking about her. I miss her, man. It was just once in a while, but it's been damn near every day the last few weeks."

"What are you going to do?"

"I don't know. Shit, I don't know..."

And the screen faded to black.

I hit the pause button and let her process what had transpired.

"I'm assuming," Savannah started after a moment of silence. I put the phone down and looked at her just as she looked up at me. "I'm assuming I'm the 'her' you were talking about."

The look in her eyes told me she was still having

difficulties wrapping her head around it, but there was just enough hope in her eyes to tell me that she was working on it.

"You are. It's also the last time I have any air time, outside of advancing to the next round, in this episode."

Savannah brought her legs up to sit crossed legged, then used her hands on either side of her to lift and shift to face me. "Why did you stay then? I'm trying really hard to believe everything. I mean..." She paused before pointing her hand toward the wall behind the bed. "I want to believe it. I wouldn't have kissed you otherwise." Ah, she was pointing to the kitchen table, not the wall. "But everything in my mind is a jumbled mess. You've never lied to me, so I know...in here, I know," she put her hand to her chest, "you're telling the truth, but I just don't understand the *why*. At the very least, why didn't you tell me?"

"You know how you say our friendship is your constant? How you don't want to ruin that, because then what do you have left?"

She nodded.

"It's the same for me, Savannah. Yeah, I have my baseball buddies and I have the guys at work, but you're my constant too. You've always been my person. You've always been my number one. And I truly believe you always will be." I reached for her hand, sitting up a little straighter. "I'm afraid of losing you. I'm afraid that we try to see where our chemistry goes, and have everything explode around us, and we fail miserably. I'm afraid that if that happens, you won't be able to be my friend anymore. Worse, I'm afraid I won't be able to handle being your friend anymore.

"But what if...what if it works? What if you're meant to

be mine, and I'm meant to be yours? And maybe that's why it's so damn hard when you're not speaking to me, or why the last three years have been strained. Because we're not following the course that's meant for us. My mom once told me that she thought you were my soulmate. She tried to cover it up by saying that soulmates didn't have to be romantic, but I feel like I met you when I did for a reason. I was supposed to be your person to get you through your storms. And you were supposed to be my person to keep me grounded.

"I want to try, Savannah," I confessed, my eyes never straying from hers. There was a slight sheen of tears hanging out in her lower lids, but she didn't let them fall. "I want to see where it goes. Because I have a feeling that wherever it goes, it's going to be great."

When she nodded and whispered, "Okay," I was shocked.

Pretty sure I fell back a little too.

I was expecting more of a fight. More of her demons to push and refuse.

"Really?"

She nodded. "Yeah. I'm... I won't lie, I'm scared to lose you. I don't have friends—"

"You do too. Shayne, Posey, Amina... Abi."

"They're friends because of work."

"That doesn't make them any less your friends, Savannah."

"Regardless," she refuted, shaking her head, "I'm terrified of losing you. But, I think...yeah, I think we owe it to ourselves to see."

I couldn't stop my smile if I tried. "And really, what

changes, other than I can kiss you whenever I want?"

She laughed, the sound watery as her eyes finally filled to the point of overflowing. After a moment though, she became serious again. "Can we... Would it be an issue if we take it slow though? Just, you know, just in case."

Just in case it didn't work.

As if taking it slow would protect her heart.

It didn't matter how fast or slow we went, my heart was already fully invested, but I'd do whatever she needed.

"I have a lifetime of years for you. We can take it at whatever pace you need."

Her smile was small, but it was real, making her brown eyes sparkle and that dimple of hers came on display. I reached up to the swell of her cheek and rubbed my thumb lightly over the indent.

"Well, what now? We're stuck here for the rest of the day..." Her voice trailed off.

"How about a movie? Something funny."

Savannah agreed, and we spent the rest of the day watching comedies on Netflix and Hulu, until finally, the sun set and she fell asleep.

On my chest.

On purpose, this time.

Before falling asleep myself, I couldn't help but think what a whirlwind of emotions today had been.

But every up and down was worth it.

So damn worth it.

CHAPTER ELEVEN

SAVANNAH

"I don't think my flight is getting out tonight," I murmured, standing by the window as Ryan put another log on the fire.

It was Sunday afternoon and so far, Southwest hadn't called off my flight. This morning's update was Denver International was trying to stay ahead of the next storm system, and hoped to have flights moving by four.

The next storm system that wasn't due to hit for another three hours.

...The next storm system that seemed to be upon us now.

When Ryan and I woke this morning, the snow had stopped, but some of the drifts were *high*.

The left side of my rental was basically submerged in snow. The only reason why the right side was visible was because Ryan's rental made a blockade for it.

We spent four hours shoveling off the porch, steps, and around the cars, but the snow was wet and heavy, and there was no way we were going to be able to manually shovel to the road.

About an hour ago though, the neighbor—from four miles down, so were they even truly a neighbor—came by with his plow and cleared the drive. We thanked him with coffee and quick conversation, where he said that if we didn't leave for the airport soon, we may be stuck another night or two.

Ryan, who didn't have a flight scheduled but was planning on buying a ticket at the airport, made the point after the neighbor left that, in the event the evening flights *were* cancelled, would I rather be stuck in an airport for the night, or in the cabin?

I'd attempted to sleep at airports before, with early morning layovers, and I'd never been successful.

So, we were hunkering down for a little bit longer, to be sure my flight was indeed going to take off today.

"Do you just want to call it?" Ryan stood from his crouch by the fire and wiped his hands on his jeans. I looked over my shoulder at him, watching as he moved easily to my side.

Sighing, I looked back out the window. "I probably should. And I have to call Conor. I'm supposed to be at the bar tomorrow night."

We hadn't talked at all today about any of the declarations that were made yesterday, but that didn't mean the affection wasn't there. Ryan pressed kisses to my forehead, cheek, temple, hand, at any and every opportunity. And while last night we fell asleep on opposite sides of the bed, this morning I once again found myself using his chest as a pillow.

So when he put his arm around my shoulders, and I leaned into the comfort of him, I couldn't help but smile softly when he kissed the top of my head. "It's just one more night. I'm sure tonight's system won't be as bad as last night's."

"It's just one more night, yes, but I didn't bring enough clothes for an extra day." I playfully spun away from him so I could retrieve my phone from the kitchen.

"I have plenty of clothes. You can borrow something."

Picking my phone up from the counter, I unlocked it as I looked up and across the room at where Ryan still stood. "I could probably wear your pants like a romper."

A cropped leg romper, but the fact still stood that his clothes were a bit too large for me.

"I'm not opposed to it." He shrugged and smirked, stuffing his hands into the front pockets of his jeans.

"Maybe I'll borrow a shirt tonight, and I'll rinse my clothes in the tub." I pulled up my contacts and put a call through to O'Gallagher's.

Three rings—while Ryan was still talking about me in his clothes—and the phone was answered.

"O'Gallagher's. This is Conor."

I crossed an arm over my chest and turned my back to Ryan, smiling. "Hey, Conor. It's Savannah. I'm not going to make it to my shift tomorrow. I'm snowed in in Colorado."

"Not a problem." The phone became muffled and I heard, "Mia. Cross Sav off the list," before he came back, "Governor shut down bars and restaurants as of eight tonight. We won't be open tomorrow anyway."

"Oh, no. I'm sorry. It's getting serious, isn't it?"

"Seems so. Brenna is working out some benefits for you guys, so if this thing lasts for a long time, you aren't hurting financially."

I didn't know how to answer that. Saying that I appreciated it sounded right, but stuffy at the same time. I had a savings, and it had a couple months' worth of expenses covered. Maybe my portion of whatever Brenna came up with, could go to someone else.

Shoot, what if this lasted longer than two months? Three months?

"Savannah."

It wasn't Conor who said my name, but Ryan, who was now by my side, rubbing his hand slowly up and down my back. "Breathe," he whispered.

With my eyes fixed on his, I took a long, deep breath in, letting it out slowly through pursed lips.

I didn't even realize that my breathing had become fast and shallow.

"Sorry, Aiden just beamed Ava with a pool cue," Conor said now, and I didn't really know why he was apologizing, but what stuck out...

"Why are Mia and the kids there today?" Mia was his wife, and Aiden, at fifteen, was more than capable of hanging out at the house with his fourteen and eleven year old sisters.

"Mia didn't want to cook dinner, and the kids wanted cheeseburger shalaylees"—they were a hit at O'Gallagher's. They were basically crumbled up cheeseburgers in a wonton wrapper, with a booze-infused ketchup—"She was here when the news hit and is helping make phone calls. Shayne came in for her shift, but she looks about three seconds from birthing that kid, so I sent her home. And she was supposed to close with Jake, but his kid is sick or colicky, he doesn't know. God, I don't miss those days."

In the distance, I could hear Mia laughing. "You do too!"

I didn't know the O'Gallagher family back in "those days," but I knew how Conor was now with his kids, and nieces and nephews, and friends' kids.

I was going to have to believe Mia on this one.

"Well, if you guys need any help for anything once I get back to town, please let me know."

"Eh. There's rumor of stay at home orders coming later this week, so just keep yourself safe and healthy. And if you hear from that friend of yours, tell him he's fucking up." And in true Conor O'Gallagher fashion, he didn't bother saying 'goodbye' before hanging up the phone.

"Conor says"—my phone vibrated with an alert, and I opened the notification—"you're fucking up." I didn't need my boss to say it was Ryan he was talking about.

Ryan was my only guy friend.

It was easy to deduce.

Especially with the end of the episode that Ryan shared with me. It came to mind and I had little doubt that it had been what Conor was talking about.

"Yeah, I think I've fixed that now," he answered, moving to stand behind me and pull me into his chest. I could feel his semi-hard state at my rear, but didn't pull away.

If anything, I relaxed into him more.

Once my notification loaded, I held my phone up so Ryan could see better. "There you have it. Cancelled. All flights cancelled through...shit, Tuesday." Sighing, I tipped my head back to his chest as I worked on rescheduling my flight. His arms stayed around me as he silently watched me.

After I submitted the change, he loosened one arm from around my shoulders and upper chest, and reached for my phone. "Can I use this to schedule a flight? I'll hop on yours. May as well get it scheduled."

Letting him, I reached up to hook both hands on his

strong forearm as he one-handedly selected and secured a flight for Tuesday afternoon.

"I should probably attempt to wash clothes in the tub. Maybe if I start early enough, they'll dry well by tomorrow." Really, I didn't want to move from this position right here, but I also knew that I had to be productive.

Had to do *something*.

"You showering tonight, or in the morning?" Ryan asked, leaning into my back—effectively pushing me forward in the process—so he could drop my phone to the counter.

"After all that shoveling? Shoot, I should have showered when we got in. I probably reek."

Then Ryan dropped his nose to the top of my head and, oh my god, sniffed.

"Ryan!" I let go of his arm and attempted to drop from his embrace, all while laughing.

He laughed too, although his ended on a groan as my back rubbed over his precarious position. Part of me wanted to be bold and invite him into the shower with me. Maybe do something about that hard-on.

But part of me was still a little bit terrified that things would change.

Again.

Even though I had the words and I knew his intentions and I saw it in his expression that he cared about me more than as just his lifelong, childhood friend, I worried that it would get old.

That he'd tire of me.

I mean, fifteen, sixteen years was a long time to know someone.

That was a lot of history.

That was—

"You're thinking too hard again, Sav." He reached out and tugged at a loose tendril of hair hanging by my ear. "Go shower. And you don't reek."

Before I could stop myself, I blurted, "Come with me."

For the first time ever, in all the years I knew him, I think I rendered the man speechless. His mouth opened, then closed, only to do the process over again.

Finally, he muttered, "Shit," before pulling me back into his arms, but this time, we were front to front. I tipped my head up and tried my best at a challenging stare, but it only made him chuckle.

"Savannah Slate, I want nothing more than to accept your offer, but I think that maybe we should wait." He visibly shuddered. "God, I can't believe I said that. I want to throw you on that bed and remind you what was so good between us, but I also need to know you're one-hundred percent on the same page. And I'm afraid you're not. Just yesterday, you said you wanted to take it slow, so now that's my intention. To take it slow with you." He closed his eyes at the last admission, as if he were afraid of my reaction.

Unfortunately, I understood where he was coming from.

Instead, I pushed up on tippy toes and kissed his chin. "I like you a lot, Ryan Madden," I whisper. Then, before it could go further, I slipped from his arms and retreated to the bathroom.

I refused to let the negative thoughts take over. Instead, every time one started, I forced it down and reminded myself of something positive—Ryan's kiss, his smile, his hug. His laugh, his nobleness, his declaration of love.

Not wanting to waste much time, I hurried through my shower, scrubbing my scalp because no matter what that man said, I was sure my hair was ripe. Eyeing my razor from my every other day leg grooming habit, I imagined that I *had* talked Ryan into the shower.

That his hard, naked body would rub against mine in the most delicious of ways.

And then I imagined his mouth dropping kisses along my neck, collarbone...taking the time to nip and suck at my breasts, only to take the kisses farther and farther down...

Yeah.

That was happening.

I turned the water a touch warmer and held the razor under the stream with one hand, while taking my other to lather my bikini line.

However it happened, whoever initiated it...

I was having sex with my best friend tonight.

* * *

Spoiler alert.

Ryan had a much stronger willpower than I gave him credit for.

When I came out from my shower in just a towel, the man cursed—*cursed*—and apologized for not getting me clothes to wear for the night.

As if that was why I was wearing a towel that barely knotted at my breast.

Because I didn't have clothes to change in to.

And I could get my hand and mind to agree on the course of action, so rather than drop my towel like the vision in my mind kept repeating, I held on to the towel tighter and smiled, thanking him for the change of clothes, before retreating back into the bathroom.

Then...THEN!...he even brought my dirty clothes into the bathroom after I was changed, to help start washing them in the tub.

I was pretty sure that the lime green thong I wore the first day I'd been here was one that I accidentally wore during a heavy period a few months ago—I typically wore my black undies during those hellish four days—where the stain just wouldn't come out.

I.

Was.

Mortified.

But the man still didn't take a hint.

Not only could he not take the sex hint, but he couldn't take the, "Yeah, I got this; you go do you, boo," hint either as I tried to move him away from the tub.

"Why don't you go find us a movie to watch while I finish this up?" I tried, a little more directly, grabbing for the unmentionables in his hand.

He lifted a brow, letting go of the nude lace bra without a fight. "You sure? I don't mind helping."

Then he reached for another floating thong, plucked it right out of the water, and wiggled his brows at him.

He was enjoying himself.

Clearly.

But it also made me laugh, so I couldn't be mad at him. I snatched that from him too. "You said no to sex. And then when I paraded in front of you in a towel and nothing else, you ignored the offer. And now you want to play with my underthings. Go." I shook my head but laughed again. "Go find something for us to watch, and I'll finish this."

Ryan stood but rather than leave, he towered over my back, putting his hands on either side of my body on the rim of the tub. Then, his voice low and his lips at my ear, he said, "I said no to the shower because I have a hard enough time being in here *after* you've showered. I ignored the offer because once we start, I don't intend to stop. And I'd rather play with your 'underthings' with my mouth. While taking them off your body." And then, heaven help me, he gently spanked my ass before standing. "But we've just restarted this song and dance. I've been hard for you for a long time. And now that you're on the same page? I'm gonna let you simmer there for a bit."

I had nothing to say to that.

And even if I did, I don't know that I *could* say anything to that.

It was my turn to be stunned speechless.

With a smile and a wink, Ryan backed out of the bathroom, tapping the top of the doorframe as he exited.

...and I could have sworn I heard his singsong declaration of loving me.

I couldn't help it. I had a stupid grin on my face as I finished my task.

CHAPTER TWELVE

RYAN

Last night was fucking torture.

Not only did I know that she *thought* she was ready to have sex again, but she spoke it with her words, and showed it with her hands.

Good god, the woman's hands...

We watched our movie, but by the end, I wasn't sure how much of the flick I could recall, because at some point her hands roamed over my stomach, and my hands roamed down her back and over her ass, which led to a pretty spectacular make out session.

I'd wanted nothing more than to use my fingers to make her come, but I also needed to stand by my word.

I wanted Savannah so on edge that when I finally took her, when we finally took that next step, she'd know without a doubt that we had *it*.

We had that thing that so many couples longed for.

We had the staying power. We had the ability to fight and love and make it through.

And hell.

I waited this long.

I could wait a little bit longer.

While Savannah slept in, I carefully left the bed to

restart the fire before heading to the bathroom to shower. I knew it was only a matter of time before I got direction from Tony, so cleaning up was a must.

Once in the bathroom, I took Savannah's clothes from their hanging spots—the curtain rod, the towel bar, and the doorknob—and quietly brought them over by the fire. After laying them carefully nearby so they'd dry further, I went back to take my shower.

While washing my hair with my three-in-one body soap, I eyed Savannah's conditioner bottle sitting on the edge of the tub.

I could do naughty things with that slick coconut goodness, I thought, rinsing my hair. Within a matter of seconds—just from *thinking* about what I could do—my cock was at full-mast.

Well.

What the hell.

I reached for the bottle and squeezed a decent amount of the white, creamy conditioner into my hand. I put the bottle back where it was, not caring if it was in the same position or not.

If she noticed it had moved and she had questions, she could ask.

Rubbing my hands together, I watched the cream disperse and squeeze through my fingers. Years ago, Savannah had been incredibly wet for me.

I wondered if she would be again...

My cock bobbed and, my eyes closing, I gripped the thickness with one hand, sliding my other down my stomach.

It wouldn't take long to meet my peak. With the smell of her hair all around me, I could imagine my best friend in front of me, her smaller hands on my cock, moving up and down...swirling at the top...her thumb playing just under the crest of the head.

My groan was low and echoed in the confines of the shower, but I held back from releasing. I didn't want the moment to end.

Not yet.

I squeezed harder.

Pumped my hand faster, focusing more on the top half of my dick and stopping just at the head.

Faster and faster. Soon, my hips began to move on their own accord, pushing into the tight vise of my fist.

Leaning forward, I slapped my hand on the shower wall, gritting my teeth and groaning.

I knew I wouldn't be able to last longer.

On a pull of my hand, I let my fist fully leave my cock, and I couldn't stop the grunt leaving my lips.

My eyes open now, I looked down at myself—red, thick, pulsing...

I tried to even my breathing, tried get it so I could work myself up all over again. Sometimes an edged orgasm was the best orgasm.

But then a whiff of coconut hit my nose again and I was coming.

No hands needed.

In fact, they were both on the shower wall as my hips pushed forward, my ass tightening.

"God. Fuck," I mumbled, watching the white cum burst from the tip. It hit my stomach. It hit the wall. And just when I thought it was through, my muscles bunched once more and another wave of pleasure burst through me.

Finally spent, I dropped my head so my chin nearly rested on my chest.

I couldn't...

I just...

Shit.

If that was the response after just *thinking* about being with Savannah again, I had zero doubt that actually *being* with her would be phenomenal.

Once my heart rate was back to normal, I cleaned up the shower and then re-lathered my own body, washing all evidence down the drain.

Dried and dressed, I wasn't sure what I would find on the outside of the bathroom door.

No worries though. Savannah was still out like a light.

She'd always been a heavier sleeper.

Now I kind of wished I let myself be a little louder in the shower.

I checked my phone at the kitchen counter for any messages from Tony, but wasn't surprised to see none yet. It was only five or so California time. Deciding to make breakfast, I took inventory of what food we had on hand.

Because Savannah had been planning on leaving yesterday, and because I generally went down to the store every five or so days, what we had was fairly minimal. I boiled up some water for oatmeal, and grabbed a too-ripe banana to add to it after, for the sweet factor.

By the time the oats were done cooking, Savannah rolled out of bed, her hair a mess around her head.

"Is there still snow?" she asked groggily, the heels of her hands in the sockets of her eyes.

"There's still snow," I confirmed, spooning more than

half of the pot into a bowl. "You want oatmeal?"

The gagging face Savannah made in response was my answer, but she followed it up with, "It's way too early to eat."

She pushed up from the bed and shuffled her feet toward the bathroom. I couldn't help but chuckle at her retreating back.

Morning person, she was not. At least, not at this hour.

Not wanting to take the full banana in case Savannah decided she wanted it, I pulled down the peel about halfway, and tore off the top half of fruit, dropping it in my bowl. I smooshed and mixed, before taking a large bite.

Not bad.

When she emerged from the bathroom a few minutes later, it was with a look of confusion on her face.

"My things...?"

I pointed with my spoon toward the fireplace. "Finishing drying by the fire. I took a shower and didn't want the dampness to affect them."

"Oh. Ok. Thank you."

I took another bite of oatmeal, watching as she moved to the other side of the room to gather clothes for the day.

"You showering?"

She looked over her shoulder before picking up another garment from the hearth. "Yeah. Wake up my head. Warm up my bones."

Immediately, an image of another way to warm up her bones infiltrated my mind, and I nearly choked on the next spoonful of oatmeal.

Savannah lifted her brows, walking toward me with her things, but clearly on her way back to the bathroom. "You okay?"

I cleared my throat. "Yep." And again. "Yeah. I am. Just...wrong pipe."

The side eye she gave me told me she didn't necessarily believe what I said, but thankfully, she let it go and was soon, once again, locked away in the bathroom.

It was going to be a long morning...

* * *

It was nearly noon when the message from Tony finally came through.

> *Here is the finale show. You'll need to log in to the webinar app no later than 5:30 pm PDT so we can check cam and audio. When you first click into the room, you'll hear feedback, but it won't go through to the Live room. Please watch the finale before logging in, as questions will undoubtedly be from the show. We'll be live from 6 pm PDT to 7 pm PDT. After the show is through, you can hang out in the room and continue to talk to others. I know Bella would like to speak further with you...*
>
> *Talk soon.*

I shook my head at Tony's continuous attempts at getting me to talk to Bella.

Bella and me...it wasn't happening.

"You wanna watch this?" I asked Savannah, even

though my eyes were still down on my phone. She sat beside me, on the bed—our couch of choice, it would seem—on her own phone, reading another romance story.

She sighed quietly. "Just...give me a couple of minutes. It just got to the good part." After her shower this morning, she seemed to wake up and even though she was reading and quiet right now, everything felt like old times.

Curious what the good part was, I put my phone down in my lap and leaned into her side—something I knew she hated.

She absolutely despised when people read over her shoulder, and I was no exception. Not ten years ago. And not today.

"Ryan!" She turned her shoulders and the phone, blocking my view as best as she could.

"Oh. It's *that* kind of good part," I teased while making an assumption—more than from her blocking my view, but from the fact that her cheeks instantly turned red—and I reached for her phone.

This time when she yelled my name again, it was on a laugh. "C'mon, man! The build up has been intense. I just want two more minutes..."

I wasn't about to stop my fight. I was curious what her favorite authors wrote about when it came to the P and the V, and their mutual joining. "If your fictional hero can get it done in two minutes, he's gotta work on his stamina." Just as I made contact with her phone though, she hit the sleep button, effectively turning the screen off.

"Now no one can read it. And poor Ford and Ashe have to wait *even longer* to get it on, because you interrupted."

"Aw, poor Ford and Ashe," I joked, but Savannah dug a

finger into the middle of my chest.

"They've been circling one another for *years*. They grew up together; their parents are friends. The chemist—"

And then she stopped.

Clear in the middle of her sentence.

Squeezed her lips together, and dropped her finger from my chest.

All so very abruptly.

"Let's watch your show."

Smirking, I couldn't let what just transpired just...end there.

"No, what just happened, Sav?"

She looked at me then, her brows up, her eyes wide open, and her face in what could only be described as hoity-toity. A face I'd expect from a royal someone or another, who just stepped in chewing gum.

"I maybe just realized," she started, looking away again, "there may kind of sort of potentially be some sort of fiction mimicking reality in this book. Just...on the level of the trope."

"And what's a trope, in these romance books of yours?" I couldn't drop the smirk from my face if I tried. I was really enjoying this moment.

"Friends to lovers. Well, almost enemies to lovers, too," she answered, matter-of-factly. "Now if we can just watch you make an ass of yourself on national television, that would make me feel a little better for right now." When she reached for my phone, the roles reversed now, I held it out of her reach.

"How does your book end, Savannah?" Still couldn't let any of this go.

It felt *right*.

This back to teasing, back to joking, back to normal version of Savannah and me that we found over the last couple of days.

And if I had a freak spring snowstorm to thank for it, I was all about it.

Thank you, Colorado weather.

"I haven't read the end of the book yet. It just released on Tuesday, and I read a different book when I got here." She reached further for the phone, her chest pushing into my arm and then rolling over to my chest. Her body was flush to mine, and I loved every moment.

"Don't be silly, Savannah Slate. How does your book end?" I tried again.

This time, I relaxed my arm enough so she could grab the phone, but with my other arm, I swept her more fully on my lap.

Startled, Savannah's eyes met mine the same moment her core met my hardening cock.

"How does your story end, Sav?" I whispered, keeping the moment silent and still.

Her breath hitched before she whispered back, "They live happily ever after. Mostly. There's some conflict of personalities but they'll love each other forever."

I winked at her. "That's what I thought," I added, before bringing my mouth close to hers.

I could leave a fraction of space between us.

I had no doubt that she'd close the gap.

But after this morning...

There was no sense waiting.

Our mouths met, the phone was forgotten, and

Savannah's hands were on my shoulders, her nails digging into my shoulders as she pressed her body closer. I wrapped my arms around her, squeezing her close.

If there was one thing I hoped would never be taken away from me, it was the ability to kiss Savannah Slate.

I didn't realize how much I missed it.

It may have only been one night, and maybe I'd let her put me to the side after, but I was older and wiser now.

This was not changing.

This being able to kiss her.

Her being able to kiss me.

Feeling her body respond to mine, and hearing the way her breath caught.

When she pulled back, I felt a physical ache.

Her hands relaxed on my shoulders, until she dropped them slowly down my chest.

"Let's watch your show," she whispered. "And maybe...maybe we can revisit this after your..." She waved a hand in the air in a circle, "finale thing."

"Maybe?" My arms loosened from the wrap, but I didn't remove my hands from her. Instead, I slide them over the small of her back until my hands encased her hips. I held her in place as I thrust my own up gently. "I definitely think it will be revisited..."

With a sassy grin, Savannah removed herself from my lap. "You're the one who agreed to taking it slow."

"I may rescind that."

Savannah laughed at that, and snuggled into my side. "Let's do this thing, then. Get it over with."

I picked my phone up from the mattress where it had fallen, and pulled Tony's last message up again. "I'm a little scared with how they might have edited it. Don't lose this warm feeling you have," I warned.

When she was silent, I looked down to find her smiling softly. "I'm good. I trust you, Ryan. I know that sometimes it maybe doesn't feel that way, and I know that my anxiety often has my mind a mess but...this was a good weekend. An even better twenty-four or so hours."

Nodding, I pressed a quick kiss to her forehead, and settled in to watch the last day of my second biggest mistake.

Thankfully, the editing of my words wasn't warped in a way that I was a total asshole. I never once used Savannah's name, nor did I go as far as saying there was someone else, but I knew that—at least, by this point—Bella had seen my closed-room phone call to Mitch.

I may not have said another word about Savannah on camera, but the viewers knew.

I remembered the last day interviews.

I remembered the things said off camera, too.

The crew tried to get me to say something about my phone call the night before, but I stayed closed lipped. One, I'd been reeling over the fact that they asked about it—it was in those moments that I knew that my phone call had been picked up and recorded. I didn't know that it was going to be used as footage though, and thought that if I didn't bow to their questions during interviewing, then nothing would be said.

Oh, naïve little Ryan.

I should have known better, and truly, had I known...

Would I have answered their questions?

Would I have blasted my feelings for my best friend on national television, potentially risking her *ever* speaking to me again?

Honestly...

I didn't think that I would have.

Hindsight being twenty-twenty, it would have been nice to have another bargaining chip with Savannah, to further prove to her that my feelings weren't sudden or spur of the moment.

Not some sort of reaction to being away and near another woman with the prospect of forever in front of me.

But when Savannah rested even more into my side, and her hand found mine, I knew that I didn't have a single thing to worry about.

CHAPTER THIRTEEN

SAVANNAH

Was watching Ryan on a streamed reality show, while sitting next to him, awkward?

You bet.

But after spending these last days with him, I could see the hesitation in him on screen. I could hear the apprehension.

All things that I don't think I would have caught had I stayed in California and forced myself to watch with his parents, or Mitch and the rest of the crew. I would have been so caught up in my own feelings and failures, that I wouldn't have seen the nervous lick of his lips when the screen went to an interview section, and, when he stayed silent, the off-camera person asking, "Who was your phone call about?"

I wouldn't have realized that the small shake of his head was about protecting *me*, rather than protecting himself.

The editing team clearly left that bit in to keep ratings up and people curious, and I wouldn't be surprised if it was brought up tonight on the finale.

The ending scene was of Bella standing on a balcony, overlooking the beach, as her red hair flowed behind her back. She dropped her head and looked down at a rose in her hand—the one she was supposed to give to Ryan, but he'd stopped her before she could—and she let go, letting the flower flutter to the ground below her as the camera faded to black.

"Well, that's a dramatic way to lead into the finale," I said, not bothering to move from my comfortable position at Ryan's side.

"They're going to want to talk about you," Ryan groaned quietly, clearly resigned.

I shrugged my shoulder, moving my eyes from where Ryan dropped his hand and phone, toward the window showcasing the winter, um, spring time, wonderland.

"You can."

I felt his chest move as he started to shake his head. I pushed back from him and crossed my legs, facing him. "Why not? I don't care."

"If there's one thing I learned through all of this, it's I value my privacy. Having your relationship blasted across televisions and all over the internet is not for me." He pushed to sit up against the headboard further. "I never could have fathomed I'd make it this far on the show. On the one hand, it was so stupid. I should have stayed and figured things out with you. But on the other hand..."

He lifted my hand from my lap.

"Had I left the show much earlier than I did, I would have gone back to California. And life probably would have resumed as normal. I kind of like that our timelines ended up here, stranded in the Colorado wilderness, in a cabin we used to be the best of friends at."

I couldn't help the smile from blooming across my face. "I think someone's been reading romance novels. That was pretty sweet."

He chuckled and tugged on my arm. "I try, I try. Now come here. I have a little bit of time before I have to clean up, and I'd like to get back to what we were doing..."

I let him tug me enough that I leaned closer to him, but didn't actually move my entire body. "Uhm, no. You could probably use a haircut before going on national television again. And a shower. Oh, and a shave. You could probably use a shave."

With his free hand, he rubbed his new, short beard. "What? You don't like this?"

"Well, I mean..." I did like it. I liked how it felt when he dropped a kiss to that spot between my shoulder and neck, and the short bristles tickled just enough. I liked how the shades-darker whiskers complimented his lighter hair, and how together, they made his gray eyes more intense.

"You should just be cleaned up some," I finally finished, unfolding myself from the bed and taking my hand back. "C'mon. I'll cut you."

His laugh was full and loud. "If I didn't know you, that would be a scary line, Savannah." He came off the bed on the same side I had, and followed me into the bathroom. "Have you cut someone's hair since you last did mine?"

It had been the summer before his senior year. We were bored and I'd told him that his hair in his eyes was driving me crazy.

And because we had no where to be but the cabin in a few weeks' time, he surprisingly let me.

I didn't do a terrible job either, if I remembered correctly. There were probably pictures of those days somewhere.

"No, but it wasn't a hack job or anything, right?"

"Nah, you're right. It wasn't terrible." He winked at me through the mirror reflection, as he stood behind me.

I took a moment to take the image in. We were a far cry from the kids who met one summer day nearly twenty years ago. No longer was he lean and growing into his body. He was big, strong, and much taller than me.

Back then, I was a disheveled girl wearing a dress her mom wanted her to wear, while her hair was falling out of a pony tail.

Today?

Today, I was a disheveled woman wearing sweats that were comfortable, with a messy bun that was crooked and looked slept in.

"Whatcha thinking about, Sav?" Ryan asked quietly, his eyes locked on mine in the mirror still. I didn't know how he did it. How he knew when my mind started to go down the path that could potentially cause a spiral.

I opened my mouth to answer, but nothing came out. Instead, I pushed my lips together and out, letting a breath out. "How do you do that?" I finally asked. "Always. For years. How do you know?"

Ryan stepped right up into my back. So close that, I either had to move forward into the counter, or lean back into him.

I chose to lean back into him.

He wrapped his left arm around my upper chest, and I watched in the mirror as he took his right hand, and brought it up to gently touch the corner of my eye. "You get tight right here when you think too hard. When your mind goes somewhere else." My lips parted and I could feel each breath pass over my lips, drying them. "And here..." He moved his fingers from my eye and instead, brought his thumb to my lower lip. "You suck in right here, right at the corner."

"I feel like you know a lot more about me than I know about you. And that's a crazy thought." I turned in his arms and looked up at him, the man, and not the reflection. "But it's a thought that makes me feel like a terrible friend."

"You know me." His voice was so low, it grumbled through a whisper.

"I know trivial things, like...your jersey number the summer you turned twelve. Or...your mom's favorite flower, because I've had to remind you when it was Mother's Day."

"You don't give yourself enough credit." He lifted my chin, while taking my hand in his other. "You know me. You just fill it with a bunch of other noise, to tell yourself you don't. Speaking of noise... What were you thinking?"

"It was stupid," I answered quietly, still looking at him. I couldn't move my eyes if I tried. He was just so...beautiful.

And I was—

"You're doing it again."

I grinned slowly in amazement and shook my head. "You're crazy."

"You're gorgeous," he responded back. I didn't know if it was because he knew what I was thinking, or if it was the first thing on the tip of his tongue. "I could spend hours watching you move, watching you dance, watching you...hell, eat. All these years, and I love your company. I love just...being with you. You say you trust me. You say that you want to change where we went wrong a few years ago. But then you close off."

"A person can have secrets," I whispered, brokenly. I felt close to tears, but I couldn't admit to him that I felt less-than when next to him.

"Sure. A person can. But relationships can't be built on secrets. And if I can tell that you're holding secrets...this will never work."

"Do *you* have secrets?"

"From you? No."

Well, shoot. Surely, he had something he kept from me!

"Actually, yeah. One."

I knew it!

I lifted my brows, curious.

"I jerked off using your conditioner this morning."

And just like that, the mood changed.

No longer did I want to cry because I was being backed in a corner, but I was crying tears of laughter. "You didn't!"

Ryan let go of me to cross his arms over his broad chest. "What of it?" The smirk on his face told me he wasn't lying...

And that he truly didn't care.

He had no qualms about it.

"Does that mean your dick smells like coconut?" I asked, laughing.

"I don't exactly smell my dick, Savannah," he answered, with a grin.

"I mean...if you didn't want us to go slow, I could figure this out..."

Ryan sobered quickly then. "No secrets, Savannah."

Sighing, resigning to my own sobering, I tipped my head to the side. "Fine. I was just thinking that you grew up so well and I... Well, I didn't. It's true when they say men age well."

"Oh, Savannah." Ryan chuckled lightly, shaking his head minutely. "Ohhhh, Savannah." He took both of my hands and pulled me flush to him once again. I was realizing I really liked being this close to him.

I'd like to be closer...

"You grew up *so* well." Ryan dropped his mouth to my ear. "So, so well." The low hush of his voice, the breathes that puffed from his lips and landed on my ear, sent chills of pleasure up my spine.

Then he was kissing my shoulder again and...

Gasping, I pushed him away.

But oh, I was also laughing.

"Did you just give me a hickey?!" I turned to face the mirror, tugging at the material at my shoulder to see.

Sure enough, a red bruise was forming.

"Ryan Madden."

This time when he pulled me back into his chest, when his hard cock pressed against my back, I had no doubts, no qualms, no second thoughts when he spoke. Even if the words did scare me a little. "I love *you*, Savannah. Not whatever version of you that you think you should be. *You.* And I have since the day I met you. You can ask my mom. And yes, I marked you. It will fade, but my love won't."

"I can't cut your hair if I'm crying," I mumbled, bringing my fingers to my cheeks to dash off the tear drops that fell from my eyes.

"Then don't cry. Not because I love you. Because I piss you off sometimes? Sure. Because you're holding a baby who has your nose but my hair? I'll probably be crying too. But not because you're my person. You're my number one, Savvy. Always have been. Always will be."

Well, that just made it worse. "Ryan!" I groaned, rolling my eyes up toward the ceiling and trying to will the tears to drain back where they came from.

When he hugged me, turning me back toward him, I buried my face in his chest. The tears slowed and I breathed him in.

I just couldn't believe the turn of events these past few days had brought. Had you told me six months ago this was where I would be, with my best friend telling me that he loved me, I'd have laughed in your face.

But to know that he returned my feelings...

"I've loved you since I was nine years old," I whispered into his chest. His arms tightened around me at the news. "I was terrified I was too young for you to hang out with when you told me you were almost eleven. More and more, little by little, you became my person, too." I forced myself to look up at him. "I just... That day... My head..."

He nodded. "I know, Sav. Just like I know your mother wasn't much help in that department. But trust me what I say—what I say is the truth. You will never have to doubt words I say or actions I take."

"I shouldn't have pushed you away."

"I should have pulled you back. There's no use with the should haves. But I also think that we're older and wiser now."

"Well, not that old and wise."

His grin was crooked as he nodded. "Truth. We've got some time still to make more mistakes and figure things out. But maybe, we'll do them together. More than we have."

"I like that," I answered quietly.

"Me too."

As much as I enjoyed standing here, wrapped in his arms...

"We're running out of time though. Take your shirt off," I demanded, turning away to open my toiletry bag. I almost always carried a small pair of shears when traveling.

One never knew when the inspiration for bangs or layers would hit...

To note though? I was pretty damn good at long, wispy bangs on myself.

"Oh, so that's what this was about. You wanted me naked." Ryan pulled his shirt off and tossed it to land on the rim of the tub.

"I've not exactly made that a secret," I chuckled, glancing up at him in the mirror. I tried to keep my eyes on his, but it was no use.

My eyes trailed down his chest slowly, and even in the reflection of the mirror, there was no mistaking his attraction to me.

"You really shouldn't wear gray sweatpants," I croaked, managing to take my eyes off his reflection, and back to my task. Shears in hand, I also grabbed a small water bottle I had on hand. "Go sit in a kitchen chair."

"Yes, ma'am."

I filled the bottle as he walked away, and it took everything in me to not watch him retreat. Satisfied with my arsenal—I also grabbed a small-tooth comb—I followed him shortly after.

We made small talk while I trimmed him up, and anytime I asked him about questions he may be fielding in a short while, he just shrugged them off.

Within an hour—because I wasn't exactly a professional, and every time I thought I was finished, I found a slight imperfection—he had a fresh, clean 'do, and when I suggested again that he shave to truly be clean cut and chiseled lines, again...he denied.

"Nope. I like it. You like it. It stays."

"Fine. Now, shower. And I need to wash my hair in the morning so... Maybe don't use my conditioner." My face was red and my heart was pounding, but I managed to get the tease out.

After a short laugh and a deep, toe curling kiss, he left to shower.

And maybe this time while he showered, I couldn't help but think of his strong hands on his thick cock.

Instantly, I felt wet between my thighs.

This was going to be a long, long night...

CHAPTER FOURTEEN

RYAN

"And we're back! Welcome to the second half of our *Rose* finale. It's the portion you've all been waiting for. We've talked to Joe, Dustin, and Hank. It's time to put Ryan on the hotseat."

Tony was having way too much fun with this tonight.

Because Savannah told me that lounging on the bed while doing this was probably not the best idea, I was sitting at the kitchen table with my phone propped up using a number of random items. Originally, we'd set me up so my back was to the rest of the cabin—which worked for me, because it meant that Savannah had to sit near me, even if she wasn't in the view finder—but then she said that it wasn't a good view.

That I needed a solid wall behind me.

To be honest, I was afraid she was going to have us do some major rearranging and move the bed to use the fireplace as the background.

Thankfully, she decided to just pull the table out from the wall enough so I could have my back to the wall and the window, showcasing the white snow outside, but not being so blinding that I was cast in a shadow.

However, I was still in enough of a shadow that she unplugged one of the lamps from the bedside, and plugged it in nearby.

She was crazily good at this lighting thing.

And while she did have the expanse of the cabin to walk about in, she chose to sit in the chair across from me, staying nearby even though technically, she didn't have to.

"Ryan, how have you been since we last saw you?" Tony asked on his half of the split screen.

Each guy he'd interviewed was placed on the right of the split screen, with him on the left. While it was clear all us guys were at home, Tony's set-up was semi-elaborate.

The guy even wore a suit.

Granted, so had Hank—but with a bolo tie. He was from South Dakota.

"I've been good, thanks for asking." I leaned into the table, which earned me a kick to the shin. I had to force myself to not shoot a playful glare at Savannah and instead, sat up straight again.

"It looks cold where you are."

I made myself chuckle, and looked over my shoulder briefly. "Yeah. Snowed in. Crazy, right? But that's March in Colorado."

"Let's talk about that phone call, why don't we?" Tony just went right in for the jugular.

"Tony. Man. You know that I won't talk about it." I said it with a grin, hoping that it didn't come across as annoyed as I was.

I mean, I was prepared for the question.

Savannah and I talked about how it would likely come up.

...Didn't make me like that it was asked.

"There have been a number of guesses on your

Instagram account," Tony continued, and I frowned.

"I don't have..."

"Is Ryan Mads seven not your account?"

"Yeah, from like...high school. I don't even know the last time I looked at that."

I glanced across the table toward Savannah, who was already on the case, pulling up Instagram on her phone. She had the device laying flat on the table top so I could see what she was doing.

I had no idea what types of pictures I'd posted that many years ago. No doubt there would be images of Savannah on it—she'd been my best friend—but there had to be pictures of other girls, too, right?

"The guesses are this blonde." Tony's face was replaced by an Instagram image of a girl I dated briefly when I was a freshman in high school. "Or this one. She's on your account a lot. Cougar. Rawr." The image changed to one of my mom and me, around my twentieth birthday.

"Really, Tony? That's my mom."

"Oh, sorry! You're a gorgeous woman, Mrs. Madden. This girl is the other contender. You guys look awfully cozy in those secluded woods..."

Before the image changed, I just knew it was one of Savannah and me from our last summer here. The summer after we found the creek. And sure enough...

"Tony. I'm pretty sure this is illegal," I said instead. "None of those women gave you rights to use their images on television."

"Fine, fine." Tony had the audacity to sound resigned. The left screen changed back to his webcam. "What happened, Ryan? Everyone wants to know. You and Bella were jiving. Everything was great right before that last night..."

"I know it's not something people want to hear, but I knew that Bella wasn't the one for me—"

"The mystery woman back home was. Is."

"It sucks that it took going on the show to figure it out," I continued, ignoring him, "and if I could apologize to Bella more, I would. It was wrong of me to stay..."

And even though I wanted to, I didn't add that I tried to leave, but that was because I wasn't allowed to. It was expressly forbidden.

Go figure, I had a list of things I was allowed to talk about, and things I wasn't allowed to talk about...but I couldn't extend a similar list to them.

"After the break, you will have that opportunity! America, we will be right back."

The signal for the commercial break came on and I slouched in my seat for just a moment before leaning into the table, away from the phone and toward Savannah.

"What did you find?" I whispered.

"Your account has blown up, Ryan," Savannah whispered back, turning her phone toward me. Sure enough, Instagram pictures that hadn't seen the light of day in *years* had hundreds of comments, thousands of likes...

"Shit. I don't even know my password to shut it down," I mumbled, scrolling through the feed.

"Who do you have with you?" Tony's voice came through my phone. "Is that your mystery girl?"

Annoyed, I pulled myself back to look into my phone. "Do not bring her up. Do not mention her."

"Tsk tsk, Ryan. You left the show and still managed to

smell like...well...roses. Does she know—"

"She does."

"You don't even know what I was going to ask."

When I didn't say anything, he continued.

I should have said something...

"Your overnight with Bella. Does she know about that?"

"She's watched the show." Still, I glanced across the table back to Savannah, who was once again looking at my Instagram feed. The image that was up was the one Tony pointed out of her and me. After a moment of staring at it, she slowly started to scroll through the comments.

I nearly said her name to get her to stop, but managed to stop, covering it up with a clearing of my throat.

"Ah, but does she know that you fulfilled your relationship with Bella that evening?"

"We didn't."

"We have footage that says otherwise."

"No. You don't."

I couldn't believe this guy. He was truly slimy, just trying to get the best story for television. It was surprising to me then that the show did as well as it did.

That no one had complained...

Oh yeah.

The contracts we signed.

NDAs—non-disclosure agreements—that lasted twenty years, the proposed life of the show. No one had been *able* to talk negatively about the show yet.

"What you have is footage of a closed door and a heavy conversation. But ask Bella. Nothing happened."

"How would your girl feel if we did ask Bella, but she told the world differently?"

If it had been three days ago, I'd be fucking screwed.

Instead, I looked across the table at Savannah. When she didn't look up from the phone in front of her, I gently tapped her with my toe. Startled, she brought her head up and stared at me with wide eyes.

"She trusts me," I finally answered Tony, watching Savannah.

Who, thank God, smiled lightly and nodded. "I do," she mouthed.

"We'll see," Tony chuckled, but then the signal for going live again sounded and once again, the finale was rolling.

This time, my camera was off, as Tony began to talk with Bella. After hitting the microphone symbol to mute my phone, I moved from my chair to stand behind Savannah's. "What did you find?"

"There are some favorable comments." Savannah scrolled to one. "'*Aw, y'all are cute! I hope she's your #MysteryGirl!*' Or this one, '*You two look like more than best friends... Love you!*'"

"Where did she get the best friends from?"

"The caption." Savannah scrolled up in one quick swipe to show me.

Ten years down. Times ten to go. Best friend.

"Did I write that?" I frowned, leaning closer.

Savannah laughed lightly, shaking her head. "No. Well, you put it in. But I told you what to write."

"Sounds about right."

I pulled her chair out and easily lifted her—startled shriek and flailing arms and all—and sat down in her chair with her in my lap.

"Ryan!" She tried to scold me but when I kissed the

back of her neck, she sighed happily.

"Hmm... You like that spot too?" I whispered against her skin.

"Little bit," she answered softly, tipping her head to the side. "Don't start something you won't finish. Or, rather...can't finish. Shoot. I said that out loud."

"I muted my mic."

"Oh. Ok. Then...go on."

Laughing against her neck, I couldn't believe that we were here.

In this moment.

In this position.

With these words...

"I love you," I said for what had to be the twentieth time today, but the sentiment wouldn't get old.

Being able to say them out loud, and knowing that the feeling was returned.

Savannah shifted on my lap so she could face me just slightly, as she whispered back, "I love you, Ryan."

Sitting like that, we scrolled through other comments; some I shook my head at, some I literally gagged at.

My mom was *clearly* my mother, America.

"Oh, I can't wait to tell her the next time I see her," Savannah chuckled, sliding off my lap so I could go back to my spot by my phone. It was only a matter of time before I'd be needed again.

Dryly, I answered back, "I'm sure she'll think it's hysterical too."

Savannah stayed standing though, when I sat.

"I'm going to go read while you finish up here. Is that okay?"

"But—"

"It's like...ten more minutes, Ryan."

Sighing, I nodded. "Fine. Back to that friends to lovers book?" I asked, wiggling my brows.

Instead of answering, Savannah just laughed and turned away, heading toward the bed. I was seriously regretting my decision to move slow...

But at the same time, not really.

I thought this was good for us.

Unfortunately, my smile was wide on my face when my screen joined Tony's and Bella's only seconds later.

Tony did his final introductions, and gave Bella the floor to say her piece to me. Nearly too late, I realized my mic was still muted, and I quickly pressed the icon to unmute.

And Bella had a lot to say.

I wasn't sure that I wanted to get something in, because I had already said my piece—on the show, to her, to Tony, to the finale... I had nothing else to add.

And Tony, clearly planning for it, didn't even give me an opportunity to correct anything Bella said.

"And that's it, folks. Thank you for watching this season of *The Rose*." He further ended it by sharing social media stats—my Instagram handle, too; I needed to figure out what to do with that account—and just as suddenly, the show was complete.

"Thank you, everyone," Tony now addressed a Zoom-conference-like screen, with all twelve men and Bella. "We'll be in touch shortly with the male that will lead the next show. Rumor has it, it's one of you twelve."

"Well, we all know it's not me," I joked, itching to turn the camera off. "It's that's all, I have to figure some travel arrangements out."

As the other guys and Bella started talking at once, I bid my final goodbye and turned the damn thing off.

I was done.

Officially finished with that chapter of my life.

Now—standing up and heading toward Savannah—it was time for the next one.

CHAPTER FIFTEEN

SAVANNAH

On Tuesday morning slowly, I woke slowly.

Before opening my eyes, I knew that Ryan hadn't woken yet—the fire was quiet, I could feel the slight dip of mattress behind me, and then...the slow deep breaths of a deep sleeper.

Gently, I rolled to my back and looked over my shoulder at him.

On his own back, Ryan had an arm thrown over his head, bunching the top of the pillow downward, and his other arm was curved slightly, allowing for his hand to rest on his stomach. At some point, he'd tossed the comforter from his upper body to rest near his hips. Even the sheet was pushed down to his lower stomach.

Here I was, sleeping in a long sleeve thermal shirt with a tank top underneath, with unattractive sweatpants on, and I was comfortable, and there he was, in a tee and shorts, getting rid of covers as he slept.

Oh, to be so warm blooded, I thought with a chuckle.

He'd always been that way.

A one-layer kind of guy, where I had to wear multiple layers to stay warm.

When you were out and about, you could always remove layers; you didn't necessarily have the ability to add them.

With that thought...

My head started to play "removing layers."

First, the layers of clothing were my own. Then, they were Ryan's layers...

And suddenly, I was wide awake.

The last thing one could ever call me was a morning person but with thoughts of Ryan's bare body over mine...

I could be a morning person with the right motivation.

Knowing that this morning was our last one in the cabin, and that in just a few hours, life would go back to normal—or so I thought—I wanted this.

I wanted him.

I wanted us.

Feeling brazen, I rolled to my side to face him, and slowly pulled the sheet down to where the comforter rested, then took both, and pulled them down to Ryan's mid-thigh area.

Through his sweatpant-type shorts, I could see the heavy outline of his cock, resting to the left. From this vantage point, I knew he wasn't full, but I also knew he wasn't completely lax. That visual person that I was, I was suddenly thinking of his cock growing to stand tall, and just like that, I could feel myself becoming slick between my thighs.

I wanted to take advantage of that near-morning-wood state of his, but wanted the full deal to be all on me...

We hadn't broached this line again though, and because Ryan was clear in his wanting to wait, I had fears of his reaction. Would he be pissed if I put my hand on him? My mouth?

My heart racing—in anticipation rather than anxiety—I made up my mind. I knew how I would go about this.

I placed my hand gently on his stomach, just under his. My thumb brushed alongside his pinky as I lifted myself toward him, so I could press my lips to his cheek.

A small kiss there, a small kiss to his cheekbone—the man had great cheekbones; it truly wasn't fair—and then a small kiss to right in front of his ear.

His breath hitched, held, and then was released with an audible sigh.

"Ryan," I whispered.

When he didn't respond, I tried again, my voice still soft. "Ryan..."

"Hmm?" He swallowed in his sleep, then his lips parted.

"Wake up?"

He said something that sounded similar to "too tired" but it wasn't clear in the least.

"I want you," I managed to whisper, even if the words felt foreign passing my lips. "Screw going slow."

"S'vannah." My name was said on a slow sigh.

"Ryan."

He "hmm'd" again, and when the arm that had been thrown over his head came to rest on his stomach with his other hand, I was afraid he was about to fall back into a deeper sleep.

Maybe my touching him was crossing a line, but I could make *him* touch *me*, right?

I sat up and removed the thicker of my layers, leaving me in my tank top. I should be chilled, but my body was overheated, needing to take this next step with Ryan in our relationship.

Laying back on my side, I brought my body as close to his side as I could, before reaching for his right hand and bringing it over his body, connecting—and holding—it with my left breast. Even though it was me who made the contact, my heart stumbled in my chest at the feel of his large hand covering me.

"Ryan. Wake up."

His hand flexed against my breast this time, and after one squeeze, he squeezed again...

And it was then that he seemed to realize something was different.

His eyes opened slowly, and he turned his head on the pillow to first, see what his hand had, and then they drifted up to mine—kneading my breast once more.

This time, I knew he was well aware of what he was doing.

"Savannah." His voice was thick with sleep but his eyes were very aware.

"Please. No more going slow." I hated that I felt like I was begging.

Ryan stared at me for what felt like minutes but was likely only seconds, before he slipped his hand out from underneath mine. The feel of his fingers brushing over my nipple had the sensitive tip coming to life. I felt both nipples tightening in anticipation.

Rather than pulling away though, he just moved his hand to my hip.

"Are you sure?"

I nodded. "Absolutely. One-hundred percent. More than anyth—"

Before I could finish the word, his mouth was on mine,

and that hand that was on my hip? He used it to roll me to my back.

This was no slow kiss.

Not a getting-to-know-you kiss.

This was a kiss that said he wanted me and he wanted to devour me.

My answering kiss said the same, and with my eyes closed, I could feel every emotion in the room.

While our mouths were fused and our tongues were meeting, swirling, dancing, Ryan brought one of his heavy thighs between mine. I spread my legs easily, wantonly.

That semi-hard cock from before was now very hard, and he pressed it just above my mound.

Not even thinking about it, my hips began to move, trying to find an angle that would allow that hardness to press against my most sensitive nerve endings.

Whether it was my wiggling or his abiding by my demands, when that hardness met my core, I wrapped a leg around his hips, trying to hold him there. I didn't move my hips again however, knowing that I was seconds away from coming. Just holding him there, the pressure against my clit, was enough to keep me wet and for my folds to grow swollen.

Ryan found my hands and held them by my head before breaking our kiss, but only so he could move those kisses down my neck, along the strap of my tank top, just over the neckline of my tank top...

And then he was gently biting down on my nipple over the cotton, and my body bowed into his.

I opened my eyes to watch, but didn't say anything.

I couldn't say anything.

Other than bring in a shaky breath and squeeze his hands.

He released one of my hands, and I watched as he brought it to the hem of my shirt to push it up, slowly. He followed the trail of cotton with kisses to my hip bone, to my belly button, up, up, up as he brought the material to just under my breasts.

Before he exposed them, he looked up at me once again. "You're sure."

I nodded. "I'm sure. Please."

First, he brought the material over one breast. I wasn't an overly busty girl by any means, but he apparently liked what he saw because after the moment of staring, he slowly lowered his mouth directly over my nipple. My back arched in anticipated response, essentially feeding him my tit.

But I needed that hot fuse over me.

Not one to disappoint, he sealed his mouth over my breast and slowly pulled back, sucking on my nipple as he did, before releasing it with a soft *pop*.

The peaked nipple pebbled tight once again, and when he brought the tip of his tongue out, I held my breath.

When he took that tip of his tongue and gently played at the underside of my tight nipple, I moaned and closed my eyes.

And when he ran his teeth gently over my nipple fully once again, I moaned his name while holding tighter to his hand.

"Other one," he then mumbled, before pushing my shirt up fully and treating my right nipple to the same treatment that the left received.

He took his time between both breasts, playing with my

nipples and sucking on my breasts. I wasn't much a breast-suckle-kind of girl, but it gave my nipples time to relax so I wasn't reaching my edge before the good stuff even began.

The more he sucked, bit, and soothed my nipples though, the higher and higher I got. "Ryan, I can't... No more. I need you. I'm wet, and I'm needy, and God, I need you."

"Will you come from nipple play?" The breath from his words brushed over a wet tip, and I nearly came from that alone.

"God, yes, I think so, but then I won't come later."

"Oh," he said with a chuckle. "You'll come later."

And then he went right back to it, releasing my hand so he could simultaneously roll and tweak my other nipple with his fingers.

Every time he brought me closer and closer to my peak, I pulled my chest down in retreat, but pushed my hips up, looking for release.

But the moment he moved his mouth, my breasts were back up, looking for the moisture of his mouth.

"So fucking sweet," he mumbled before closing his mouth around the nipple he'd last been tweaking with his fingers.

This time, when he bit gently on my nipple, he also rubbed the tip of his tongue over the tip in quick motions, and then when he pinched my other nipple tightly...

"Ryan!"

My pussy clenched and pulsed, as my thighs pushed and bracketed his hips. While I knew I was wet before, I knew that I was soaked now.

There would really be no need for further foreplay, because my channel was more than ready for his cock, even if I knew I wouldn't come again. Just feeling his thickness in me again...

I couldn't wait.

While I remembered that last night, the memories were fading and I needed to feel him once again.

Ryan suckled my breast lightly as my body calmed, and when my legs relaxed fully at the sides, he brought himself down and dug his fingers into the top of my sweatpants, pulling them down.

Not having any reason to stop, I lifted my legs up to help him bring the material off of my legs.

"No panties?"

"Not when I sleep."

His grin was wicked. "Noted."

The sweatpants were forgotten somewhere on the floor and Ryan took my thighs in his arms before lowering his body to the bed, his face...

"Ryan..."

"Shh. I need to taste you."

This was not something we did last time. I would have remembered the sight of his blond hair between my thighs.

I'd have remembered the feel of his breath on the sensitive folds.

And when he brushed his tongue from opening to clit...

Oh. I'd have remembered that.

My body once again bucked up and if anything, Ryan simply held my thighs tighter to his head, as one hand kneaded my skin and the other moved to rest above my mound.

My moans weren't soft now. Every time his tongue played with my clit, or he sucked it into his mouth, I was louder than the last.

And when he dropped his one arm from my thigh so he could push a thick finger into my pussy?

Oh, I could be heard then.

"Ryan! Ohmigod, Ryan."

He was playing my body like he knew it intimately—and I supposed, to an extent, he did. But the way his mouth ate at me, and the way he'd earlier sucked at my tits to get me to reach my peak, made this all feel like it was meant to be.

He played me in ways no other man had done before.

My body responded to his ministrations in ways it never had before.

The mere fact that I was nearing another orgasm was proof in that.

Whenever I played with myself, it was almost as if my clit retreated after coming the first time. If I had the patience and the time—which, when it was your going to bed activity, you generally had time just not maybe patience—I could eventually get myself there again, but never as quickly as Ryan was doing now.

I was getting closer, and I wasn't shy in telling him. "Ryan. Almost. A little... A little more..."

If he just put one more digit in me, I knew it would be enough.

Instead, with one finger still pumping lazily inside of me, his mouth released my clit and he kissed up my middle, to my breast, and bit down on my nipple once.

My body jerked and my channel tightened around his finger, but it wasn't quite enough.

Before I could complain though, his mouth was on mine

and this time, his kiss was slow.

Lazy.

Loving.

And the finger in my pussy slowed too, turning upward to slowly rub the upper wall of the muscle.

Gently, he slipped his finger out of my sheath and I moaned into his mouth.

"So close," I whined.

He pressed a quicker kiss to my mouth before pushing up from the bed. "I know."

There I was, laying mostly naked but for my tank top pushed up over my boobs and stuck by my arms, sprawled out like a wanton woman at a brothel, and he was *leaving*?

"Where are you going?" I pushed to sit up, pulling the tank top down. Before I could get it all the way down though, he was leaning against the bed with one fist to the mattress, and pushing the shirt back up.

"Take it off all the way, Sav." Then, not even bothering to turn his back, he took off his shirt and pushed down his short in quick succession, his cock bouncing free from its earlier confines.

It was huge, and thick, and the vein along the underside was strong and proud. The head of it was mushroomed with a nice domed shape and, oh, that drop of precum...

He grabbed hold of the thickness with one fist and called my name again. "Your shirt, baby."

Shaking my head from my stupor, I did as he asked, tossing it toward the rest of our clothes.

With his cock still in hand, Ryan turned toward his bag and came back with a foil wrapper.

Thank god, he was thinking straight, because I would

have just let him push inside. I was that ready and needy for him.

He kneeled at the edge of the bed and arranged my legs to his sides, before making work of the condom. His cock was quickly sheathed and soon, he was leaning over me, pushing me to my back.

I could feel the head of his cock at the top of my pussy, and I reached between us to push it down, closer to my entrance.

"No take backs," Ryan said, eyes locked on mine. "No mistakes, no regrets. I love you, Savannah." His eyes pinched at the sides when I notched the head to my entrance, showing he was just as on edge and ready as I was.

"I love you too, Ryan. Just... I need you. Please." I kept my fingers on him, holding his cock in place.

Then, no room for second thoughts—not that I had any—his mouth met mine as he pushed his cock inside.

CHAPTER SIXTEEN

RYAN

It truly was like coming home.

Feeling her tight walls surrounding my engorged cock was like no other.

I'd had fuck buddies before Savannah and after Savannah, but I was determined that there would be no more.

The night of her twenty-first birthday would be just a blip in our radars, because now, there was no going back for me.

This was where I belonged.

In her arms.

Her eyes locked on mine as my body elicited reactions from hers. Feeling her channel flex and pulse around my cock, making room in the tight confines of muscle.

There were no words anymore, just my grunts being answered by her moans, our sweat mixing, and the sound of her readiness as my cock thrust in and out.

We kissed long and hard, short and sweet. I bit her ear; she bit my shoulder.

I suckled her breast, she held me closer.

Her pussy grew tighter, and I knew that she was close to another orgasm and I couldn't wait to feel the rippling of pleasure surrounding my cock, making her channel tighter.

Suddenly needing it, I brought a hand to her clit and began to flick the bud.

"Ryan..."

I rubbed it in circles.

"Oh!"

I used the tip of my finger to strum the underside.

"Ryan!"

And there she was, her body arching and her pussy pulsing. I pushed and held my cock in to the root, holding there and gritting my teeth as the feel of her tight muscles tried coxing a reaction from me.

When her muscles released just enough, I pulled my body up to be kneeling between her thighs, and began to thrust quickly and deeply, not pulling out more than half way before pushing back in again. These short thrusts caused her chest to bounce and when Savannah brought her hands to her breasts and squeezed them...

"Fuck, Savannah."

I leaned forward on my fists, my thrusts still powerful, spreading my own thighs to bring hers wider.

She let go of her breasts, causing her nipples to brush my chest, and reached for my ass. Then, when she kneaded before digging her fingers into the muscle...

"Ugh!" My ass tightened as I pushed deep inside her one more time, my cock jerking in her channel as I came. I jerked twice more before collapsing on top of her, spent.

Knowing I was much larger than her, I used whatever energy I had left to roll us over, bringing her to rest on top of me. However, the action had my dick slipping from her warmth, and I wanted to cry at the loss.

Savannah kissed my chin lightly. "That was..."

"Amazing." My voice was still thick from passion. "Undeniably so. We fit, Savvy."

Her smile was small but she nodded. "We do." Then she pressed another small kiss, but to my lips this time. "How about that shower you didn't take me up on the other day?"

"Stupid of me then. Not making that mistake again." Before she could push off of me, I had her wrapped in my arms and I moved us so I could stand. Her laugh in my ear had my smile growing from ear to ear.

And when she wrapped her arms around my neck, still laughing, I knew...

This was my forever.

She was my always.

* * *

Hours later, and I was afraid that things were going to change again.

I was afraid that Savannah wanted this morning's events knowing that we were going back to San Diego and back to our "other" life.

But screw that.

My life lost its brightness once before, when Savannah pushed away the first time; it wasn't going to happen again.

When I walked her to her apartment door, I wanted nothing more than to ask to come in with her.

But I also knew she likely needed time to process. She'd need time to be with her thoughts, and sort through everything.

It's not like last time. She's not pushing you away. You've smiled, and kissed, and held hands for the last six hours. You laughed and joked and made love twice this morning. This is not like last time.

"You'll call if you need anything?" I asked, adjusting her back pack from my shoulder, down to the floor.

Her smile was wide. "I'm literally doing laundry and then going to bed. We'll talk tomorrow. Go sleep in your own bed."

I'd slept next to her for the last four nights; I didn't know how I was going to manage to sleep in my own bed, without her, tonight.

"I love you," I said softly, squeezing the hand I still held.

"I love you, too, Ryan." She went up to tiptoe to kiss me, and I brought the kiss a little deeper, a little more indecent.

She laughed when she pulled away. "I'll see you later, Ryan."

I let her go, watching the door shut quietly behind her, before making my way slowly, lonely, down the hallway, toward my own apartment.

Mitch and I lived on the same floor as Savannah, but clear on the other end. Where she was in a smaller one bedroom with a balcony, we had a two-bedroom san balcony.

I used my key to enter my place, not at all surprised with how quiet and dim it was. "Mitch?"

When he didn't answer, I figured he was at the hospital or out for the moment.

With my phone beside me the whole time in case Savannah needed me, I got back to normal life.

CHAPTER SEVENTEEN

SAVANNAH

The world was officially going crazy.

It was Thursday and California had an amazing surge in cases of this new virus, and we now found ourselves under stay-at-home orders. To be honest, every time I watched the news or opened up a social media app, I became more and more scared of what was going on.

I'd even had my groceries delivered yesterday, because I was afraid of going out to the stores! And I was too much of a control freak to let someone else do my grocery shopping.

Yesterday, Ryan had come over for a little bit and we watched a new Netflix movie, but the more I was hearing, the more I felt that I should probably "social distance" from him too. He was, after all, living in the same apartment that a frontline worker lived in.

Granted, Mitch hadn't been home, but if his schedule was anything like it had been in the weeks prior, he would likely be home for the weekend before heading back in on Monday morning.

Also, knowing Mitch and having been to their apartment when Ryan was away, I knew Mitch wasn't the cleanliest of guys. I mean, the apartment wasn't trashed by any means, but I seriously doubted the guy was Lysol-ing every counter and door handle when he was home.

And now Ryan was back and could potentially be bringing whatever viral-bugs they had at their apartment, over to mine, and...

Yeah.

This was a recipe for disaster in my anxious mind.

I'd texted Ryan earlier in the day to suggest that we stay in our respective apartments, and I knew he didn't take it well. Rather than reply via text, he came over and knocked on my door.

When I didn't let him in, he was visibly upset.

I tried to assure him this wasn't like last time, I wasn't pushing him away, and eventually I got him to listen to my concerns—not that he was thrilled about the direction of my thoughts, but he went back to his own place and now, here I sat, in my bed with my phone, wishing he'd just call me.

I needed to hear his voice.

Maybe I should have invited him over.

Maybe he should be hunkering down for this order, here. I mean, we'd been together for four days before coming back to California.

I was lonely without him, which was a funny thing to think, considering I'd been pushing him away for the last however many years.

But four days was seemingly all it took to crave his company again.

Just as I started to open his contact, a Google Duo notification sent my phone ringing and his face was right there.

Smiling, I answered the video call.

"I miss you. I'm sorry," I said, immediately.

"I miss you too. Mitch is going to be home in an hour

and says he wants to discuss some things. I guess he's been sleeping at a hotel during the week."

"I've been thinking that maybe it would have made more sense for you to come here..."

Ryan lifted his brows and his smile was slow and crooked. "Really? You thought that?"

"I mean, yeah. Because it's not exactly fair that you have to live with the potential germs, and we *were* together right before the order was in place, so it kind of makes sense that we could hunker down together. But now you've been there, and I feel like maybe the point is moot."

He was shaking his head. "Nope. Never moot. Let me talk to Mitch and see what he's been dealing with. I'm sure it sucks to be hanging out at a hotel when your apartment is only a few blocks away. But he knew I was going to be home this week, which was why he did it. I guess a few of the other fellows and residents have been doing it too. Staying at a hotel."

"Okay."

"Besides, I miss sleeping beside you."

"I'm sure you don't miss my anti-morning-person quirks."

"I've recently discovered a way that you can be a morning person though." His smirk was enough to get me shifting in my seat.

Because it was true.

While it was only one morning thus far, it seemed to be a great way to get me to wake up and be fully with the program.

"I miss what you do to my body," I whispered. "My toys just aren't the same as your mouth and fingers."

"Savannah Slate, do you have a dildo?"

"Mm. Yes. One that has rabbit ears, another that's generally too girthy but does nice things to my clit, and another that's supposed to be a sucker but it doesn't do much of anything for me. Especially now that your sucking is so fresh in my mind..." I could see in the viewfinder that my face was flaming red, but other than the embarrassment of talking to him about unmentionable toys...

I wasn't really embarrassed to talk about what he did to my body.

"Fuck, I'm hard."

"I'm wet," I admitted, shifting once again.

"Hold that thought." He was up and moving, and I heard the click of a lock before he went back to where he was. In all the movement, I was able to gather he was in his bedroom.

"Will you touch yourself for me, Savannah?" He asked, his voice low and throaty as he went back to his bed.

"Mhmm." I nodded and slipped a hand under the band of my leggings, under my thong, and found my clit. I was certainly wet already, and my fingers were able to rub over the slick nub easily.

I'd never done the phone sex thing, so I stayed quiet even though I wanted to moan.

"Are you touching yourself?"

"I am."

"Don't be afraid to let me hear those breathy sighs of yours."

"Okay." I continued to rub my clit in soft circles, biting my bottom lip. Watching him watch my face was a turn on itself. His pupils became dilated and his mouth parted. There was a shift to the camera then...

"Are you touching yourself?" I asked, bravely.

"Fuck, yes. Next time, it will be your hand. Your mouth. I want your pretty lips surrounding my cock, Savannah. Your tongue swirling the tip. I want... Shit, I want to see you. Not just your face."

"I... Just... How about..." I removed my hand from my pants and put the phone down on my bed.

"Where did you go?"

"One second!" In my closet was a two-by-two cube organizer that I hadn't been using but never got around to taking apart. I moved to the foot of my bed before grabbing a couple of paperbacks to stack.

Then, picking the phone back up, I propped it against the books so the view finder had a clear view of my bed.

"I can't believe I'm doing this," I laughed, but I was in need of an orgasm, and the ones I had last night with my toys just weren't good enough. "Is this okay?" I asked, leaning into the bed and dropping my head so I could look into the camera.

"Fuck yes, it's okay."

He was suddenly moving too and if I had to guess, he's propped his phone up on his dresser, because now all I could see were his hips. He was wearing sweatpants again, that did nothing to hide just how turned on he was.

I pulled my leggings off and sat back on my bed, my thighs spread wide.

That was...

Never a sight I'd seen and never a sight I wanted to see again, I thought, focusing on the smaller of the video screens.

"Shoot, Ryan. That's... No." I closed my thighs and moved off the bed again.

"Savannah Slate, get your ass back and show me that beautiful pussy." His face was in his camera now, and he looked ready to stomp down the hall and throw me back on the bed.

"I need to shave, Ryan!" I reached for my pants.

"You do not. Now, *please*. C'mon. Help a man out. I only have like...thirty more minutes before Mitch is back. Go back to the bed. Please. I want to watch you get yourself off."

I battled with the thought.

"Savannah..."

"Fine. But only because I'm horny."

"That's the best state to be in, when I'm here, ready for you."

"I'm regretting my spontaneity," I mumbled, putting myself back into position. What seemed like a great thought before, now seemed juvenile.

Not that I was having video chat sex as a teenager, but it just seemed like something the Snapchat era did.

"Don't think about you. Listen to me. Watch me stroke my cock. You want your hands on my cock?"

Ryan was really good at this, I thought absently, before deciding to hell with it, and going all in.

"I wanted to suck you the other morning," I confessed, putting my fingers back on my clit and rubbing soft circles. "But I was afraid of how you would respond. Waking up with my mouth on you."

"Shit. Fuck, Savannah." I watched his hand tighten on his shaft. "Next time, do it. Kay? I just almost fucking came from that alone. I've been imagining your mouth on me for days. Fuck, months. Years, if I'm being completely honest. And that would have been a fantastic start..."

"Was it not a fantastic start to your morning?" I teased, shifting and spreading my legs further.

"It was. God, yes, it was." He was pumping his cock now, occasionally bringing his palm up over the head to gather the moisture there. I wanted to study the way he got himself off. I wanted to know what he liked so that when it was finally my turn, I'd satisfy him.

"Dip your fingers into your pussy."

"Yessir." I spread my fingers and slipped my hand down until my middle finger breached my entrance. I bit my bottom lip as I pushed the finger inside. It was odd, focusing on what I was doing and feeling, while watching his hand work his cock.

I wished that I could see his face like he could see mine.

I vowed that while this may not be the only time we'd do this, we were doing more of the in-person sex too.

Ryan continued to give me direction, and soon I found my own voice and asked him to do things to his cock, too.

In a matter of minutes, I was pumping two fingers into my pussy with my other hand rubbing my clit, and I was seconds away from coming.

Needing that release, I squeezed down on my fingers, and the feeling of the fullness from my fingers and the action to my clit, and I was there.

"Oh!" My hands stilled as I felt my body throb around my digits. When I pulled my fingers out slowly, they were followed by thick cum.

"Fuck, that's gorgeous. It's... Shit. Lick your fingers," Ryan demanded and if I hadn't been curious about it once before, many years ago, I would have probably balked at the idea.

Instead, I brought my fingers to my lips at the same time I changed positions so it was my face in the camera, as I lay on my belly, and sucked my fingers into my mouth.

Then Ryan was grunting and I could see as his cum came up to decorate his abs.

"Fuck, I need to shower," he groaned, and I couldn't help but laugh.

I was happy, and free, and it was Ryan who brought me there.

It had always been Ryan.

"Stay right there. Like that..." And then his hands were moving toward the camera before he said, "Fucking gorgeous."

"What did you just do, Ryan Madden?" I demanded, although there wasn't a lick of heat in my words.

"Screenshot."

I gasped, but realized that in my position, there really wasn't anything to see. I had an arm folded in front of my chest, and my other hand was up by my face. At the time, I'd been laughing.

Clearly, if someone saw it, they'd realize I was naked but...

"No one sees that," I said, even though I knew that Ryan would never dare to share something that personal with anyone else.

He'd moved his phone now so that it was focused on his face. "If you think for one second I'd ever willingly let another person see you like this, you're out of your damn mind, Savannah. You're mine. You're my person, my love. I hope you enjoyed whatever dick you got before me, because it's only mine that's going in that pussy from here until forever."

I should have been concerned about the words he spoke. Sure, in some of my romance novels, they came off as sweet and caring. A true alpha type thing to say. But in some, where the context was different, it was borderline abusive.

But I knew Ryan.

And while these words weren't anything like he'd ever said to me before...

"The same goes for you, Ryan. I won't tolerate cheating."

"As if I'd ever cheat on you." He shook his head. "I finally got you where I've wanted you for years. I'm not about to let that go."

"Okay."

"Okay."

Then I smiled, and he smiled, and all was right in the world.

"I'm going to shower. And then talk to Mitch. I'll be over around dinner time. Does that work? I can order something to be delivered?"

I nodded. "That sounds good. I should shower too. And maybe make room for you."

"Long-term room," he suggested. "Not just a drawer, but maybe...a couple of them."

I liked that.

I liked it a lot.

CHAPTER EIGHTEEN

RYAN

I was riding a high and on cloud nine.

The woman I loved, loved me too, and we were minutes away from playing house for the foreseeable future.

"You're sure that's ok? I don't want to put you out," Mitch said, standing at the kitchen island. He showered at the hotel and changed into clean clothes before coming, but had laundry to do before his next shift in thirty-six hours. He was adamant about staying six feet away, so I stayed on the outskirts of the kitchen.

"No, you've been here by yourself for the last few months and now with everything going down, I don't want to put *you* out by you staying at a hotel. I'll keep paying my half of the rent, so don't worry about that—"

"I wasn't," he chuckled.

"—but then you don't have to spend extra on the hotel, even if the hospitalists are covering a fraction of the costs. Savannah and I are good."

"I can't believe you were at the cabin when she got there. Talk about timing..."

I couldn't agree more. "I'm glad she went. And I'm glad I was there."

"You two have gotten your heads out of your asses

then?"

I shrugged a shoulder and grinned crookedly. "She loves me."

"Anyone with eyes could see that. The fact that you didn't was annoying as fuck."

"Why did you sign me up for the show then?" I was genuinely confused. If he knew that Savannah loved me, and he'd had ideas that I was hung up on her...

"Shit or get off the pot, man. That's why. It knocked you around some, did it not? Made you realize what you hadn't been paying attention to?"

On that note, he was right. "True."

"And, further, it got Savannah to confront her feelings, right?"

"True, again."

"Great. Then go live with her for a bit while I work with this virus. We've had younger people coming in with symptoms and it's truly scary. Makes me wish I'd stuck to baseball."

"They postponed the season though, so you'd just be stuck at home with the rest of America. Hell, the world."

"After dealing with what we've been dealing with, and it's only the beginning, I almost envy the sitting around, stuck at home. Anyway. I'm going to shower. Again. I can't shower enough, it feels like. I'm guessing you're heading to Sav's soon?"

"Yeah, the food I ordered should be arriving to her door in about twenty minutes."

"Awesome. See you." And with that, he pushed away from the counter and went to his half of the apartment.

I was just pulling my large suitcase out of my room and

to the front when there was a knock on the door.

"Impatient, much?" I asked, laughing, as I opened the door, assuming it was Savannah.

"Hey, Ryan," said not-Savannah.

Stunned, I said nothing for a solid ten seconds. "Bella. What are you doing here?"

She shrugged a shoulder while keeping her A-list, quiet smile on. "I was in LA for the finale and thought I'd drive this way to talk."

Considering that was a two-hour drive on a good day...

"We didn't get a chance to on Monday night," she finished.

"Yeah, I was... I had..." I took a breath. "Look, Bella. I tried to leave the show. I told the producers that there was someone else, but they didn't let me remove myself from the competition. Shit." I realized we were essentially having this conversation in the hall, which could result in me being sued, so I let her inside. When the door closed behind her, I moved as far from her as I could, without being rude. Then, I laid it all out on the line for her, not mincing any words. "I've been in love with Savannah since I was a kid, and I was having a hard time with things with her."

"I didn't think you'd been in a serious relationship... You told me you hadn't been," Bella asked, confused.

And she was right. One of our first conversations, I'd told her I had never been in a long-term romantic relationship. My longest one was maybe a year, year and a half, but that was it. It never got to moving-in territory.

"It's...complicated."

Not missing a beat, Bella then asked, "Is Savannah the best friend, then?"

I nodded, not surprised that she caught on. Being an actress, she did a lot of people-studies. She'd told me one of her favorite courses in college—because her parents wouldn't let her just move to New York City or Los Angeles without some type of degree—was human psychology.

"She's my best friend, yes. I've known her since I was ten."

"That's a long time."

"It is." Not wanting to waste time with small talk, I continued, "I am so sorry that took the spot of one of the other guys who may have been a better choice for you. If I had realized earlier in the process, I think they would have let me go, or I would have found a way to discuss it with you, but as it was, I was stuck between a rock and a hard place. You're a lovely girl, Bella, but—"

"You love her. I get it." Bella's smile was still soft but genuine. "I do. I'm sorry that I came all this way. Tony or the rest of the crew wouldn't get me your contact information, but Tony did slide me your address. I really should have left well enough alone. You were pretty clear about the fact you had someone else. I was just... I don't know, hoping that maybe that wasn't the case."

"I'm sorry," I apologized again, just as the front door opened and my name was called out before the person on the other side could see.

At Savannah's voice, I immediately stood tall. "Sav."

The door opened fully and she stepped in. Her eyes initially landed on mine and her smile was wide, but it was just after that when she realized there was someone else in the apartment with us.

Immediately, everything on her face dimmed. "Oh." She

frowned and I just knew every moment of us talking and working through her anxiety where she and I were concerned, were now being thrown out the window. "Oh," she repeated, looking between Bella and myself. "I'll just... I'm sorry for interrupting." Her voice was dejected as she turned away.

"Savannah!" I took a step forward but rather than letting the door swing close on it's own, she pulled the door closed behind her and I couldn't grab it fast enough.

"Fuck."

"That's her, isn't it?" Bella asked.

"Yeah. That's Savannah. And fuck...I... I'm sorry. I have to go." I grabbed the door handle and swung it open, not even bothering to wait for Bella to leave.

I had only one thing on my mind, and that was catching up to Savannah.

She had to have run down the hall, because I could hear the heavy closing of a door that could only be hers, as I didn't see her down the hall. I followed after at my own clipped pace and was thankful to find her door unlocked.

"Savannah!" I called out, just as another door shut.

Shit.

"Savannah. It's not what you think..." I went to her bedroom and tried this door, but found it locked. "Fuck," I mumbled, resting my forehead to the six-panel door. "Savannah, listen to me. It's not what you think. I promise you. C'mon, baby, unlock the door. Please."

When she didn't—and instead, I heard the shower start, because of course, she would retreat to the shower—I stepped back from the door.

This was not ending like this.

She could have her minutes in the shower. Hell, she could have an hour or more in the shower. But we were confronting this. She was going to know that she couldn't jump to conclusions.

That she *shouldn't* jump to conclusions.

I didn't know what the fuck else I could do to prove to her that it was *her* I wanted, short of a proposal! And if me staying with her for the duration of this virus had taken her a couple of days to wrap her head around, she certainly wasn't ready for *that* question.

Resigned for the moment—other than popping the lock and breaching her privacy, I had nothing else to do at this moment—I walked back through the one-bedroom apartment toward the front door, seeing the bag of food that must have been delivered while I was talking to Bella.

I'd told Savannah I'd be here before it got her so of course, the food arriving and my *not* arriving would have prompted her to come check on me.

I wasn't going to let this stop me. I wasn't going to let her shut me out.

I was going to head back to my place to grab my things, and I would sit it out, waiting for her to come to her senses and talk to me.

Back at my place, Bella wasn't anywhere to be seen, but Mitch was sitting on the couch.

"I heard you just had a little bit of a snafu in your plan."

"Don't joke about it," I growled, moving to my suitcase, still standing where I'd left it. "Do you know how many fucking circles I had to talk around earlier in the weekend? And every time I thought Savannah was there and trusted me again, she'd get caught up in her head again, and we were starting over. I really thought we got past all that." I moved to bring the suitcase closer to the door.

"Does she talk to someone?" Mitch asked, genuinely curious.

"She does." He didn't need to know that she'd been talking to someone since we were young, and he didn't need to know all the little things that made her head go into that space.

"That's good. You going to go talk to her?"

"I'm going to go fucking camp out in her apartment until she realizes that I'm not fucking going anywhere."

Mitch laughed. "You are so far gone, brother. Calm down. She doesn't need you to go all alpha male on her."

I thought about her books for a moment then took a deep breath. "Sometimes I think she does need that. You're good here? If you need anything, holler. Otherwise, I'll keep up with my rent like discussed and I'm going to go try and figure things out with Sav."

"You're good. Go. Go win her back. Although, I don't really think you've lost her. It wasn't like you were making out with Bella when she got here."

I frowned briefly at his correct assumption. "How long did you and Bella talk for?" Because surely that was the only way he'd known.

"Just long enough for me to know she felt sorry for causing the scene. And to get her number."

The laugh that passed my lips was unexpected, but felt good. "You would. See you," I added, shaking my head and dragging my suitcase out of the apartment that had been my place to rest my head for the last three years.

When I got back to Savannah's, I was relieved to find

that the door was still unlocked. I pushed it open and propped my suitcase by the wall, before shutting it and engaging the deadlock. I didn't plan on going anywhere, and I knew Savannah would refuse to go anywhere in the current climate.

We were settling in for the long-haul.

Listening closely, I could hear that the shower had shut off. So, I brought my suitcase closer to her bedroom door, and left it along the wall before going to sit on the couch.

I didn't turn on the television though.

I wanted to be fully aware of when she moved from her bedroom, into this room.

Thankfully, it didn't take long before she emerged from her bedroom, hair wet and wrapped up in a clean bun, with her hands held nervously in front of her.

She wore loungewear and couldn't look more beautiful.

I moved over on the couch and patted the seat beside me. "Let's talk."

CHAPTER NINETEEN

SAVANNAH

"Let's talk."

His words were calm, but I wouldn't have blamed him if he were upset.

I'd resorted back to "Last Week Savannah" and allowed that damn devil voice to speak louder than the voice of reasoning. I didn't just leave him—I freaking *fled* his apartment.

He had every right to be upset with me.

"Savannah," he said gently when I didn't move from my spot. "Please come and sit with me."

"I'm sorry," I said, before even moving. "It was just..."

Ryan stood then and came to me instead. He gently pried my fingers apart so he could hold my hands.

"I love *you*," he said softly, looking into my eyes. "You have to believe that. You have to trust it. Or else we're doomed before we even begin."

"No, I know." I was nodding my head with tears threatening, but I squeezed his hands. "I know. Just, after the high of the day and the weekend, it all just kind of came to a halt. It was really hard hearing you tell Bella my words, and then walking in to you and Bella talking, it brought all those feelings back again. And I know it was childish to run rather than confront it. You. Her. All of it," I added with a quick roll of my eyes, which allowed tears to drop over my lower lid. I groaned and tried to brush them away, but Ryan wouldn't let go of my hands. "I called my therapist. I'm going to do an emergency session with her at the top of the hour. I just...need to talk to her."

I was on the verge of telling him that I was sorry I couldn't talk to him, but he wrapped me in a hug. "Good. I'm glad. And if you need me, I'll be right here. I'm not going anywhere, Savannah."

Wrapping my arms around him too, I hugged him tight. "Thank you. For understanding."

"Savannah Slate, I've walked many miles by your side. I get you."

I didn't answer him, but that was because he knew that I knew.

He knew me.

Just like I knew him.

And I was starting to trust that that was enough.

RYAN

She chose to set up her laptop at the kitchen counter, but told me she didn't want me to hide away in the bedroom. She wanted me to stay. I sat by her side as she joined the mini-chat room she'd be using with her therapist, and when she asked me to find a notebook for her, it was only then that I got up to leave.

By the time I got back with the pink college-ruled notebook that had been in her bedroom, the screen was open and her therapist was in view.

"You must be Ryan," she said, with a kind smile. "I've

heard a lot about you over the years."

I moved my hand awkwardly in a side wave, as I put Savannah's notebook down and resumed my seat at the stool beside her. "That's me. I've heard a lot about you, too." I'd never sat in on one of Savannah's sessions—the majority of them had been done in person, but for maybe a handful for some reason or another—so I'd never actually *met* her therapist, but outside of Savannah's friendship with me, and her familial relationship with her father, her therapist was the one person who had been in Savannah's life for many years.

"Savannah says she's comfortable with you being here for the duration of our session, and I told her what a big step that was for her. I know you are one of the few people she trusts, but to bring you here is a big deal."

While I knew that she wasn't being judgmental in the least, I felt like she was warning me. This was a big deal. I knew from many of the times Savannah came over, post-sessions, that they wrung her out emotionally. Even if the session was only thirty minutes long, she would be nearly comatose afterward, and just wanted to veg on the couch.

We did that often in our teens.

Just sat in silence with one another, with a stupid show on the television.

I don't think I realized then what a big deal it was, for her to come over straight after a session. But as we got older, and I started to put pieces together—she wasn't quiet because she was sad, but because she was tired; she wasn't tired because she stayed up all night, she was tired because of a therapy session—I took thrill in the fact that when she needed those moments to decompress, she came to me.

"I only want what's best for her," I admitted. "And over the years, I made some bad judgement calls in that direction. But we spent the weekend working them out."

"So I've heard. All right, Savannah. You called because you said you had some moments you wanted to talk about. How are you feeling now, knowing that we're going to get into them?"

I sat quietly at Savannah's side, watching and listening, not interrupting. When she got to the part about Saturday morning, when our first major wall in our friendship was brought up, I was surprised to realize her therapist had no idea that Savannah and I had been together, romantically, once before.

I knew for a fact she talked to her therapist about everything. Even after that night and things between us were strained, I could always tell when Savannah had a session, even if she didn't come to me for the decompression anymore. So, the fact that she left out that one night spoke loudly to me. I wanted to know why it hadn't been brought up before?

Shame?

Embarrassment?

I watched as Savannah continued to speak about the weekend, and also about Bella and the show. I watched how she kept her hands folded tightly in front of her, or picked up a pen and mindlessly began to bounce it before putting it down roughly. Then she'd hug herself.

But not so much a hug-hug, but a folding in on herself.

And then when she started to cry when she was relaying a story, it was me who was fidgeting in my seat, because I wanted nothing more than to hold her.

"Ugh!" She said with a laugh, brushing her cheeks with her palms. "I so did not think that was going to happen today. I was feeling so good too. I didn't think I was going to cry," she laughed again into the camera.

"It's okay...!" Her therapist truly was a kind, soft-spoken woman, and I liked that Savannah had her. "I think that what you've been doing is reverting to some old thinking patterns."

Savannah nodded. "I know. I'm really great at jumping to conclusions."

"And we know that that stems from trying to be someone your mother wanted you to be."

"I...I heard from her today," Savannah then admitted softly, looking over at me from the corner of her eye. She swallowed before looking back at her phone. "She called shortly before I went to Ryan's, and saw him with Bella."

"Ahh." Her therapist nodded her head ever so slowly. "Do you think maybe that's the reason why you had been on one plane where Ryan was concerned, and then it switched unexpectedly?"

Savannah nodded, and in the viewfinder, I could see her look up and stare at a random spot in the kitchen. "Yes. But I was so wrapped up in my head and being fifteen again, that I didn't take the time to go through my steps to realize I was in one of those negative thinking patterns."

"And now you're reflecting on that. It's okay to have missteps, Savannah. You know this." She went and explained a couple of different ways Savannah could work around this, and once the session was through, and everyone gave smiles and goodbyes, I didn't waste a second pulling Savannah off her stool and into my arms for a tight hug.

"I love you," I whispered into her hair as she wrapped her arms around me, standing between my thighs.

"Thank you for being here. For not giving up on me," she whispered back, and I squeezed her gently in response.

"Never giving up on you. Let's go chill on the couch with our now-cold food, just like the old days."

Savannah pulled back from my hug and gave me a beaming smile—even if her eyes did look exhausted. "I'd love that."

CHAPTER TWENTY

SAVANNAH

SIX MONTHS LATER

"Ryan?" I spoke gently, turning my naked body into his.

It had only been a few minutes since he gave me the best orgasm of the week—it was only Sunday though, so he had a lot of opportunities to change that—but I was ready to do it again.

Unfortunately...

The man was asleep.

I laughed lightly, adjusting my arms so I was laying comfortably on my side, and ran a finger up and down his abs.

We gave up condoms a few months ago, but the problem with that was after an intense orgasm, Ryan was liable to fall asleep. Whereas before, he still had to get up to dispose of the spent condom.

That was okay though.

I'd much rather feel him bare between my legs, feel him fill me with his seed—I was on the pill though, so no baby Savvys or Ryans. Not yet, anyway—than to go back to before.

These last six months had been amazing.

The stay-at-home order lasted longer than anyone truly expected, and even when it was lifted in phases, many people chose to stay at home for a while longer yet.

In that time, Ryan and I accomplished a lot.

First, with the support of Ryan, my dad, and my therapist, I finally cut ties with my mom. Too many random phone calls that would send me spiraling, I was proud to say that it was my idea to get a new number and go unlisted. I reset all of my social media profiles to private, too, which also worked in mine and Ryan's favor because, even though the next season of *The Rose* was nearly complete, viewers were still flocking to my social media accounts for a glimpse of Ryan—who finally, fully, deactivated all of his unused accounts.

Second, we officially moved in together.

At the end of Ryan and Mitch's lease, they decided it was best if they didn't resign for another year. Besides, Ryan was still hunkering down with me, unofficially moved in, and Mitch had his new girlfriend—a funny story in itself. Maybe we'll tell you someday.

My lease was due to expire in three months, but Ryan and I had already discussed doing the grown up, real couple thing, and started to look at starter homes near our parents' houses.

If that didn't say forever, I didn't know what did.

Then finally, in the third major accomplishment of our young lives, the O'Gallagher siblings were opening a second location, this one in the Gaslamp Quarter, and asked us to be the managers.

Life had been a whirlwind with Ryan by my side.

From the day I moved from Ohio and met the boy on the bike, he'd been a constant presence in my life.

It took us some time to work through bumps, and

honestly, I wouldn't change a single moment of our journey.
...and it was only just beginning.

EPILOGUE

RYAN

FIVE YEARS LATER

"But it's mine!"

Three-year-old Noah Madden was *not* a fan of sharing.

Well, he had been fine with it before Sadie started to steal cars and trains from his hands while he was trying to build a new track.

These days, sharing was not very high up on his list of priorities.

"Gemma came over to play with you, remember?" I spoke gently to my son, kneeling in front of him while holding the toy helicopter he'd ripped from Mitch's daughter's hand only seconds before.

The little redhead had cried, running to her mother, but I didn't blame her. I'd had this particular helicopter ripped from my hands before by the headstrong boy who looked just like me, but with my wife's darker hair. It didn't feel good to have the plastic blades cut against the palm of your hand.

For the most part, Noah was a good boy, but man oh man, was he independent and liked things to go a certain way.

I never realized a young child could be so particular.

"But. It's. MINE!" When he reached for the toy again, I

loosened my hand around it—not wanting that specific injury again—but rather than play with the toy, Noah tossed it across the room.

"Okay. That's fine." He knew we didn't tolerate throwing toys. "Time out."

Then the screaming pursued and while I took his arm and brought him back to his bedroom in this one-story ranch Savannah and I bought five years before, I felt like to the outside world, it looked like I was dragging him.

And the way he was carrying on, it sounded like I was hurting him.

Then he flipped his body so I truly was dragging him along the concrete floors, kicking his heels along the way.

I kept my calm though.

I kept my cool, even with annoyance coursing through my body. No one prepares you for this demon side of the product of your loins.

Thank god he'd never had temper tantrums as a much smaller child, or else we probably wouldn't have thirteen-month-old Sadie. Granted, we also thought he had the temper tantrums *because* of Sadie. They kind of mimicked the ones she would throw when she didn't get *her* way.

We were a house full of headstrong toddlers. Joy.

In his room, I set his timer and placed the small white rectangle at the top of his dresser where he couldn't reach. "Three minutes. And then when you're ready, you can come out and play nicely."

That was answered by another demonic scream, and I gently closed the door to it.

Closing my eyes, I took a deep breath before going to join my wife and my best friend's wife, walking into the wide spaced living room.

Mitch was working at the hospital today, so it was just her and their two-year-old Gemma today.

Now, instead of playing with Noah, like had been the intention of this get-together, Gemma was getting her hair braided while the wives spoke quietly together.

On Savannah's breast, Sadie was clearly falling asleep.

Noah had only nursed for a year, but Sadie was holding on a little bit longer. Savannah was determined to let her nurse as long as she wanted, but Savannah was also hinting at having another baby and I didn't see her nursing through her pregnancy.

Not with how the last two had made her uncomfortable seven of nine months.

"Let me take her," I interrupted, reaching down to take Sadie.

"You only want sweet snuggles to make you feel better," Savannah teased with a smile, reclipping her nursing cami and putting her sweater back in place.

"You're right. I do." No sense denying it. I leaned down to kiss Savannah once before bringing our daughter to her nursery—which had been a small office before we brought Sadie home—closing the door and drawing the curtains, slowly and quietly to not disturb her.

Once the room was darkened, I turned on her white noise machine and sat in the rocker. I maybe closed my eyes for a minute too, loving the quiet atmosphere.

I could hear Noah's timer going off in the room next door, but I didn't hear his door open yet. He'd be out soon, and I was probably going to have to play bad cop again.

Not that Savannah didn't, but she was bad cop

yesterday, and it wasn't her favorite role.

It wasn't my favorite role either but I'd do it for her.

Sighing, and more than happy with this life we'd built, I looked down at my sleeping daughter and took in her tiny features. She looked so much like her big brother, but with a daintier nose and lighter hair. Sadie was definitely the feminine version of me.

...and because we had two kids who looked like me, I had zero doubts that when Savannah was actually ready for round three, I'd be happy to oblige.

I wouldn't mind another little girl, but one who looked like Sav. Or even another little boy, but who took after her.

At the sound of Noah's door cracking open, I stood gently and moved to lower Sadie into her crib. Just as her back hit the mattress, she opened her brown eyes sleepily and gave me a wide, full-toothed smile.

"Love you, Sadie girl," I whispered, putting her blanket on top of her.

She reached for her stuffed dog and pulled it into her chest, before closing her eyes once again.

I left her room and met Noah in the hallway. "Are you ready to play nicely?"

He nodded with a sniffle.

"I think you should go tell Gemma you're sorry for hurting her."

He nodded again and giving me a sad smile. "Okay. I'm sorry, daddy." Then he was off, racing to the family room, no longer the show of a desolate little boy, but a happy kid whose best friend was in the room.

I followed behind, and found Noah pulling a puzzle out of a chest. "It's Lightning McQueen! You can help me,

Gemma."

Together, they poured out the large puzzle pieces and began to work on the oversized floor puzzle, and I sat down beside my wife, pulling her into my side but not interrupting her conversation.

Not much later, the front door opened and Savannah's dad walked in. Puzzle forgotten, Noah raced to him and talked his ear off, and shortly after that, Mitch walked in too.

The only people missing were my parents, but they were on a Route 66 motorcycle trip, and would be returning Monday.

Just in time to help Savannah and me move into a bigger house.

Promptly at the one-hour mark, Sadie woke up from her nap and together, five adults and three children, we piled into cars to go out to dinner. On the way home, with two sleeping children in car seats, I held my wife's hand in silence.

"I love this life," Savannah said softly, rolling her head on her seat so she could look over at me. There was still just enough light outside that I could make out her features, and I brought our connected hands to my lips to kiss her once.

"You're my number one, Savannah Madden."

"You're my number one, too. Are you ready for this next chapter?" She asked just as I pulled into our driveway, the headlights illuminating our For Sale/House Sold sign.

"More than." I squeezed her hand and lowered it, gently maneuvering the car into the single-car garage.

I wasn't going to miss this.

I was excited for the new build with the three-car garage and four bedrooms. The one that sat on a three-quarter-acre lot, versus our small postage stamp lot.

I was excited for the barbeques and the company, and our kids having room to run.

And for Sadie to have an actual bedroom.

Once parked, before she could unbuckle and we would start to get the kids out, I leaned over the console to take her face in my hands. "Each chapter with you is better than the last."

"Just like my romance novels."

"Happily ever after, baby."

WHAT'S NEXT?

FOR THE FIRST TIME

7-16-2020 (or earlier)

CHAPTER ONE

ELODIE

You know those post-apocalyptic movies?

Where the actors rush through the empty grocery store, and grabbing whatever cans they can get their hands on while the world is literally falling apart outside? And they're throwing everything into their shopping carts? Practically sweeping their arm along the shelving in an attempt to get in and out as quickly as possible, while avoiding the zombies that claw at the sliding doors?

Yeah.

Those movies.

I am now realizing just how fictional those movies are.

I mean, zombies aren't real, I know that.

But the cans would have been *long* gone by the time the world shut down.

How do I know this?

Because Scottsdale isn't even on lockdown and the only things you can buy are sweet potatoes, one container of eggs, and plant-based chicken nuggets.

Not a single can of soup lined the shelves. Hell, not even

broth.

Pasta...

Heck, pasta's been off the shelves for nearly as long as the toilet paper.

And while I love those cute baby chicks my favorite author shows on her social media, I still preferred to eat real chicken versus some plant-based thing disguised as chicken.

I make my way down the next empty aisle slowly, trying to decide if I can make dinner out of the single bag of quinoa I found.

I can.

I just...

Don't really want to, I think with a sad sigh.

At this rate though, beggars couldn't be choosers, and it looks like I'm eating quinoa this week.

All week.

Joy.

My phone rings in my hand, and upon glancing down, I see my big brother's face.

Actually, I see up Ryder's nose.

Smiling, I answer the Google Duo request and bring my phone up for a brief moment so he can see my face and not the warehouse-type ceiling of the store. "Hey, big brother."

The screen moves as he picks up his own device, and no longer am I looking up the nose we both have—his is bigger though—and instead am looking at his face. "Good, you're up! I wasn't sure if you would be sleeping today." I'm a night NICU nurse, and work twelve-hour shifts. Usually, I'm only scheduled three times per week but currently, while the world is going crazy with the novel coronavirus, I'm not working as much. Heck, I'd be lucky if I wasn't asked to take a leave of absence, due to the hospital losing so much money with the lack of elective surgeries.

"I worked last night but took a nap this morning. Figured I'd attempt grocery shopping." I flip the camera on my phone and show him the aisle I'm in. "It's not looking too great for me today." I turn the self-camera back on and put the phone down on the toddler seat of the cart.

"Yeah, that's what it looks like here too. It's a good thing mom did her regular Costco bulk run at the end of February. Jordan and I were running low on TP and she hooked us up."

Jordan, who I haven't met yet, is Ryder's roommate. I've heard a lot about him—they're both motorcycle mechanics and work in the same shop—but when you live eight-hundred miles away from home, you don't often get a chance to meet the people coming in and out of your family and friends' lives.

"Still with the roommate," I tease. "When are you going to get your own place?" I'd think at twenty-eight, he'd be ready—heck, I thrived in my own place, and I got it right after graduating with my Bachelor of Science in Nursing—but he's been splitting rent with someone or another since the day he moved out of the house.

After high school, it was to move in with his then-girlfriend, Jae. I liked her...until I found her making out with someone who *wasn't* my brother.

Picture it with me:

Twenty-first birthday. Your girls and you moving around Olde Town Arvada, hitting the tap rooms and having a great time.

And then seeing the woman who your brother proposed to just the day prior, playing tonsil hockey with a man who was *not* your big brother.

Fun times.

And I was sober enough to record it, but drunk enough to send it to my brother, damning all consequences.

It was the first time in as long as I could remember that my big brother—my very best friend in the whole wide world—wouldn't talk to me.

It took a good five months for him to even acknowledge me, as if it were somehow my fault that the woman he'd wanted to spend the rest of his life with didn't want to be monogamous with him.

That was hard.

Really fucking hard.

Harder because while I'd been home for my twenty-first birthday, I was going to school in Tempe, Arizona, so after a great weekend gone bad, I took a plane away from Arvada, Colorado, and had to figure out how to get through the next semester without my weekly check-ins from my best friend.

Anyway.

I digress.

After he kicked Jae out, he moved in with a guy named Jack, and they roomed together for two years until Jack put a ring on his girl's finger.

From how the story goes, Jordan was a new hire at the bike shop and had been couch-hopping. Ryder needed a roommate; Jordan needed a *room*...

Bingo. Both parties happy.

"Not everyone likes to pay fourteen-hundred a month for a roof over their heads."

"You could move away from Arvada. Maybe in the city?"

"I'm minutes away from the light rail," he replies, completely ignoring my suggestion but I know why—he's not the biggest fan of downtown Denver. Not so great memories there.

I turn into the next aisle and nod, conceding. "That's a good point. For those nights you decide to have a little bit of fun."

My brother isn't the biggest drinker, but when he does drink, man oh man, watch out. He's a fun drunk. Not mean, but funny.

But also funny in a way that people don't always realize he's intoxicated, so knowing he has a safe way home...

I may be the baby sister and five years younger than him, but I like knowing he's safe. I need him around for many, many more years.

"Speaking of a little fun," he says, and I see in my lower peripheral as he moves from wherever he is in his place. "Jordan and I wanted to invite you to a quarantine happy hour."

My brows go in and my lips quirk to the side. If I had the ability, I feel as if my facial muscles are attempting a right-brow up expression. But I'm not that talented, and instead, both brows are definitely doing...something. "Exactly how do you do that, when you're on stay in place orders and the restaurants are on delivery only? AND! Let's not forget I'm here, and you're there."

"New Image Brewing Company has online ordering. We ordered a whole bunch of shit and had breakfast burritos. Something about they can't sell alcohol without selling food too, so, boom, breakfast burritos."

I'd heard places doing alcohol carry-out here in Arizona too, but hadn't ventured to trying it. Granted, I'm not a big drinker. I like my girly Malibu and diet Coke. Every now and then, especially in the summer, I like a good vodka lemonade.

But really, beyond that?

I could leave it, in the take it or leave it scenario.

"So, anyway. We have the brews at our place. You don't *have* to drink to go to happy hour. Just…pick up some pretzels or something, and join the get on the Houseparty app."

I turn into the next empty aisle, no longer looking for anything specific because it's clear I won't find anything that I truly want. "All right. When and where?"

"Do you work tomorrow night?"

"I do. Tonight's my night off, and then I'm back for three in a row." Due to staffing and hospital money needs, I was going to be working "princess shifts", ie, four hour shifts. They weren't my favorite, and I'd much rather work one twelve hour shift than three four hour ones, but it was what it was.

"Jordan!" Ryder yells out. I quickly drop my hand into the cart seat and over the earpiece of my phone, glancing around to see if anyone is staring, but everyone seems to be in their own little shopping-during-a-pandemic world.

"Jesus, Ryder. Warn a girl," I murmur to myself before lifting my hand. "Maybe not yell next time?" I tell him.

His grin tells me he doesn't care.

I continue down the aisle and when I spot a single tub of Swiss Miss—with marshmallows—I scoop it up.

The weather may be in the upper seventies, flirting with eighties, these early April days, but a girl had to have her comfort things.

As Ryder talks over his shoulder to who must be the roommate—not that I can see him—I stifle a yawn and keep pushing the cart. My gait is slow, as if I'm actually browsing the shelves, but there's not a damn thing here to browse.

Just like the last ones, the next aisle isn't exactly exciting either. I just hope I don't have to attempt another grocery run at another store. My cart isn't exactly looking like today is a grocery day.

More like a, "pick up what I can to get through the next twenty-four hours" kind of grocery trip.

"All right. Tonight," Ryder says, turning back to the phone and therefore, virtually, to me. "What's a good time for you?"

I stop in the middle of the aisle but no one is around to care, and pick up my phone to speak more face-to-face with him. "Can you give me a couple of hours? Maybe three? I think I'm going to have to go to another store when I'm done here. I have quinoa in my cart, and quinoa salad and quinoa breakfasts just aren't going to cut it."

"Absolutely. Three hours. We'll set up the room, and I'll send you the link. Just join when you're able. Cool?"

I nod. "Cool," I mimic with a grin.

"See ya, sis." And just like that, Ryder ends the call.

Shaking my head while smiling, I put the phone back down in the cart. Happy for a moment.

But then take in the empty shelves and my empty cart, and sigh once again.

God, I hope this doesn't last...

FROM THE AUTHOR

Surely you've noticed a theme with Lost Without You, and my next release, For the First Time.

Like Savannah Slate, I often struggle with anxiety. Typically, I don't realize something has affected me until much later, and that was kind of the case when March 2020 rolled around. It would be a couple of weeks of forcing this introvert to stay inside, and not allow her to write at the places that words actually flowed from, before I realized I was having a difficult time.

So, rather than continue to push ahead on projects I'd been teasing for months (Unexpected and Love You Forever; they're still coming, just not as soon as originally planned) I changed my creative drive to a way of healing. A way of coping.

That's what this and For the First Time have been for me. A way to deal with COVID-19 and the world as it is.

I tried to keep sensitive to the issues. As one popular meme states, we're not all in the same boat, but we are all in the same storm. How I cope with things may not be how someone else copes. How I react, may not be how someone else reacts.

I hope that you were able to find some enjoyment in this story. I hope you were able to block out the noise and focus on a growing love.

On that note...

This was my first major release since 2018. I know. I can't believe it either. It's been a weird sort of two years, where I struggled with writing. I found myself forcing stories and I knew my readers (you!) and my characters deserved better. I'd try to write here, I'd try to write there... I had really good days and I had really bad weeks.

In the end, I'm so glad that former readers have stuck by my side, and new readers: welcome to the party! I'm so glad you're here. I have a lot planned for the next five or so years...!

Until next time...

Mignon

ABOUT MIGNON MYKEL

Mignon Mykel is the author of the Prescott Family series, as well as the short-novella erotic romance series, O'Gallagher Nights. When not sitting at Starbucks writing whatever her characters tell her to, you can find her hiking in the mountains of her new home in Arizona, or trying to tame her sassy (see: stubborn) mastiff-lab.

Connect with Mignon online:
website | facebook | instagram @mignon.mykel
Sign up for my Newsletter

LOVE IN ALL PLACES *SERIES*
full series reading order

Interference **(Prescott Family)**
O'Gallagher Nights: The Complete Series
Troublemaker **(Prescott Family)**
Saving Grace
Breakaway **(Prescott Family)**
Altercation **(Prescott Family)**
27: Dropping the Gloves **(Enforcers of San Diego)**
32: Refuse to Lose **(Enforcers of San Diego)**
Holding **(Prescott Family)**
A Holiday for the Books **(Prescott Family)**
From the Beginning **(Prescott Family)**

Caught in the Act
Homewrecker
Lost Without You
For the First Time

Trust
(an Everyday Heroes world title)

Serendipity
(a Salvation Society world title)

MIGNONMYKEL.COM

Made in the USA
Middletown, DE
03 March 2023